THE CHRISTMAS STRANGER

Books by Keith Donnelly

Donald Youngblood Mysteries
Three Deuces Down (2008)
Three Days Dead (2009)
Three Devils Dancing (2011)
Three Deadly Drops (2012)
Three Dragons Doomed (2014)
Three Daggers Dripping (2016)
Three Divers Deep (2017)
Three Doorways Dark (2022)

Youngblood Stories
Moving Target (2020)
The Christmas Stranger (2022)

A YOUNGBLOOD STORY

THE CHRISTMAS
STRANGER

KEITH DONNELLY

HUMMINGBIRD BOOKS

Kingsport, Tennessee

Hummingbird Books
A division of Harrison Mountain Press
Kingsport, TN 37660

Designed by Todd Lape / Lape Designs

Library of Congress Cataloging-in-Publication Data available

ISBN 978-0-9993667-5-2

Printed in the United States of America
by Maple Press, York, Pennsylvania

To: Olivia, Hannah, Jordan, and Caroline

The rewards for being parents,
hopefully good ones, are grandchildren.
They are like Christmas presents.
We are blessed with four. All special, of course!

CAST OF CHARACTERS

Major Players

Don Youngblood—Private investigator, FBI consultant
Mary Youngblood—Don's wife, police officer, the
    blond Wonder Woman
Billy Two-Feathers—A Cherokee Indian, Don's
    original partner
Big Bob Wilson—Mountain Center chief of police,
    Don's longtime friend
Roy Husky—Jack-of-all-trades with a shady past,
    president of Fleet Industries
T. Elbert Brown—A wise old veteran and retired
    TBI agent

Supporting Players

Gretchen Graves—Junior partner in Cherokee
    Investigations
Joseph Fleet—Chairman of the board of Fleet
    Industries
Dr. Evan Smith—The Youngbloods' family doctor
    and friend
David Steele—Associate deputy director of the FBI,
    Don's part-time boss

Cameo Appearances

Doris Black—Owner of the Mountain Center Diner
Anthony Rizzo—Trailer park manager
Linda Street—The blond beauty across the highway
Clarence Cutter—Retired medical examiner
Wanda Jones—Medical examiner, Mary's best friend
Danny West—A Native American deputy in Santa Fe
Adam Church—Senior pastor at Mountain Center
    Methodist Church
Jim Doak—Fleet Industries pilot

Very Special Guest Appearance

Jeremiah James

THE CHRISTMAS STRANGER

There are more things in heaven and earth,
Horatio, than are dreamt of in your philosophy.
—William Shakespeare

Be not forgetful to entertain strangers; for thereby
some have entertained angels unawares.
—Hebrews 13:2

PROLOGUE

The stretch of North Carolina highway in front of the James house, where Jerry lived with his parents, was notorious for speeders. Perfectly straight and smoothly paved, it tempted drivers, male and female, young and old, to push the fifty-five-miles-per-hour speed limit. Homeowners residing in the clump of houses to the right and left of the two-story stone-front house owned by Pastor James and those across the highway complained loudly and often to the county sheriff's office about speeders. Most of the time, the complaining occurred because a cat or dog, often a family pet, had perished by a hit-and-run from a speeding car or truck. The road ran straight into town for two miles. The fifty-five speed limit was lowered to forty-five a few hundred yards to the left of the James house, but that seemingly did nothing to slow traffic.

The sheriff sent a deputy out every now and then when funds in the county coffers were running low, and after the deputy wrote a number of tickets, traffic slowed down for a while. Then things went back to normal, and the whole cycle repeated itself.

On this particularly beautiful August Saturday, Jerry James was throwing a football with Skip

Carter, the kid next door and backup high school quarterback. School had just started, and so had football practice. Jerry, a starting defensive back, was fast and could really catch the football. Skip used him to practice pass patterns in Jerry's massive front yard. The James house sat at least a hundred yards back from the highway, and if you were inside, you couldn't hear the traffic. What Jerry and Skip did hear that day was the squeal of tires, a thud, and then a car speeding away out of town. Jerry knew the awful sound of an animal being hit. He turned quickly, dropped the football, and ran toward the road. The car was gone.

At the edge of his driveway, he spotted Daisy, Linda Street's border collie, lying near the centerline. A car slowed, passed the dog, and kept on going. Jerry ran into the highway silently praying, *Father in heaven, please don't let Daisy die.* He knelt and caressed the dog. Blood was coming out of Daisy's mouth, and she wasn't moving. He heard a scream from the other side of the road.

"Daisy! Oh, no. Daisy! Oh, God." Linda Street was nearly hysterical.

"Get your dad!" Jerry shouted. "She needs to go to the vet right now."

Linda ran to her house. Drivers were slowing for a brief look and then moving on. Jerry removed his sweatshirt, wrapped it around Daisy, and gently picked the dog up and started walking toward

Linda's house. Jerry was almost certain Daisy was dead. A driver stopped in front of him and blew his horn. Jerry ignored him.

"Please, Lord, don't let Daisy die," he whispered.

As he got to the edge of the driveway, he heard a car engine start. Seconds later, Mr. Street appeared in his sedan with Linda in the front seat. Linda got out and opened the back door. Jerry gently laid Daisy on the backseat, and as he did, Daisy opened her eyes and looked at him. Linda had already returned to the front seat.

"She's alive," Jerry said. "Go. Call me later." He slammed the door, and Mr. Street sped away.

✦ ✦ ✦

Skip witnessed the whole scenario from the edge of Jerry's driveway. *Jerry is crazy*, Skip thought. *He has to be crazy to run out in traffic to save a dog that's probably already dead.* But he had to admit, it would be worth it to get close to Linda Street. Linda was a blond beauty—head cheerleader, homecoming queen, lusted after by almost every boy in school. Incredibly, she wasn't stuck up. She had a smile and a kind word for everyone. And she was a straight-A student. Miss Perfect.

Jerry ran back across the highway to where Skip stood.

"Alive or dead?" Skip said.

"Alive, I think."

"If that dog lives, you're going to be one big hero," Skip said. "At least to Linda Street."

"I didn't do much," Jerry said. "Just got the dog out of the road."

"Are you kidding? You acted fast and took charge. If that dog lives, Linda is going to love you."

Jerry laughed. "Come on, let's run some more patterns."

"I'm serious, man. You should ask her out."

"That would be taking advantage of a bad situation. I can't do that," Jerry said. "Besides, she's a senior and I'm a sophomore. Senior girls do not date sophomore boys."

"Just because your father is a Methodist minister doesn't mean you always have to be Mr. Goody-Goody," Skip said.

"Shut up and throw me the football," Jerry said.

✦ ✦ ✦

That night at dinner, Jerry's mother said, "Linda Street's mom called to tell me what a brave son I have."

"And why is this?" Jerry's father said.

Jerry told his father what happened to Daisy and what he had done to try and help.

"Well, that was a very good deed," his father said. "I'm proud of you, son."

Jerry beamed. His father, although a minister, was a distant man who rarely gave out compliments. Most of his praises came as a result of Jerry's prowess on the football field.

"It was nothing," Jerry said. "Pass the gravy, please."

✦ ✦ ✦

An hour after dinner, there was a knock at the back door. Jerry opened it, and there stood Linda Street, glorious as ever. She took Jerry's hand, pulled him toward her, and kissed him full on the mouth.

"Daisy is going to be okay," she said. "You saved her. I am so grateful and so proud of you. The vet said she was lucky not to be hurt more. She seems fine."

Jerry was stunned. What had just happened? Had Linda Street actually kissed him? "It was nothing," he said. "I'm just glad I was there."

"I'm glad, too," Linda said. "And I'm sure Daisy is glad. I've got to run. Dad is waiting in the car, and Mom's holding dinner. She's going to wash your sweatshirt and get the blood out. See you in school."

✦ ✦ ✦

Jerry did see Linda in school. She would smile and say hi but never mentioned Daisy or the kiss—the kiss that he replayed a thousand times.

The following week when he saw Linda in the hall, Jerry said, "How's Daisy?"

"Oh, she's fine," Linda said. "Good as new. She won't go anywhere near the highway now."

"That's good."

"Got to run," Linda said. "See you later."

Well, what did I expect? he thought. *She's a senior and I'm a sophomore.*

Time passed and things returned to normal for Jerry. The football team had a winning season, made it to the playoffs, and won a couple of games before being eliminated. Thanksgiving and Christmas came and went. Winter was cold and snowy. Spring came and with it an explosion of new life. Jerry got a job with Parks and Recreation coaching Little League baseball. He was great with kids, patient and encouraging. His team finished first.

Linda Street was busy studying and exploring colleges. She had been offered academic scholarships at a number of schools and was having a hard time choosing. But she had not forgotten about Jerry. She thought of him often. He was blond, tall enough for her, and really good looking. What a shame he was a sophomore! One night, she talked to her mother about Jerry and told her how she felt about him.

"He seems very mature and grounded for his age," her mother said. "Nobody is going to think less of you if you date a sophomore boy, especially one as good looking and athletic as Jerry James. Besides, why do you care what anyone thinks? No regrets, okay?"

✦ ✦ ✦

One warm spring day while Jerry was in his front yard mowing, he saw Linda run across the highway and walk up his driveway. Puzzled, he stopped the mower.

Linda walked up to him and said, "How're you doing, Jerry?"

"Great. How about you? Picked a school yet?"

"I'm fine," Linda said. "I've decided on Harvard."

"Harvard, wow! Ivy League," Jerry said. "Congratulations." He wondered why she was in his yard talking to him. He just wanted to prolong their conversation as much as possible. Every second with Linda Street was priceless.

"Thanks," she said, pausing. "Jerry, I was wondering if you'd like to be my date for the senior prom."

Jerry was dumbstruck. He could not have heard what he thought he heard. "I don't understand. You're asking me? Anyone would love to be your date to the senior prom."

Linda smiled widely. "Is that a yes?"

"Well, sure," Jerry said. "That would be great."

"Thanks," Linda said. "It's in a couple of weeks. I'll let you know what I'm wearing."

"Okay," Jerry said.

"Want to go out Friday night?"

"Sure," Jerry said.

"Great. Got to run," Linda said. "I have a test to study for. Call me. The yard looks great, by the way."

He watched her go back down the driveway, run across the highway, and disappear around the side of her house. *What just happened?* he thought.

✦ ✦ ✦

Senior prom night arrived, and Jerry's stomach was doing somersaults. His mother told him the reason he needed to know what Linda was wearing was so he could pick out an appropriate corsage. His mother had gotten together with Linda's mother and decided on that.

"Jerry was honored that Linda asked him to the prom," Jerry's mother said.

"Your son is very handsome," Linda's mother said. "And such a nice boy. Linda is very excited that he said yes."

"She cannot be any more excited than Jerry."

"They'll make a handsome couple," Linda's mother said, and Jerry's mother agreed.

Jerry had turned sixteen in April and had his driver's license. His father had bought Jerry an old Jeep, and Jerry loved it, but tonight the good reverend gave his permission for Jerry to use the family sedan.

Jerry picked up Linda at her front door and was speechless. Linda looked absolutely gorgeous.

"You look fabulous," he said finally.

"You're not so bad yourself," she said. "No one would ever know you're a sophomore."

Jerry laughed. "Except everyone knows," he said.

"Well, there's that," Linda said, and they had a good laugh.

In the car on the way to the high school, Linda said, "I'll be dancing with other boys, and you should dance with other girls, but the slow dances are for you."

"Sounds good," Jerry said. *Actually, it sounds great,* he thought.

✦ ✦ ✦

The prom was everything Jerry could have hoped for. He danced with a number of senior girls, all of whom asked him. He danced every slow dance with Linda, who snuggled closer as the evening wore on.

Around ten-thirty, Linda said, "Let's slip out of here. I'll go to the ladies' room, then meet you at the car."

"Okay," Jerry said, confused. He thought they were having a good time. *Why does she want to leave?*

In the car, Linda said, "Let's go to the lake. I know a good spot."

"Sure," Jerry said. *At least she doesn't want to go home*, he thought.

At the lake, Linda said, "Kiss me, Jerry." Jerry had not kissed a lot of girls, but with Linda's expert guidance, he was kissing like a veteran in a matter of minutes. Things were heating up inside the car. He was getting aroused, and so was Linda. Within minutes, most of their clothes were off. Jerry was both excited and scared at the same time.

"Maybe we shouldn't do this," he said.

"You're a virgin, aren't you, Jerry?"

"Yes," he said without thinking.

"That's okay," she said. "So am I. We'll lose our virginity together."

Well, I have to lose it sometime, Jerry thought. *And who better to lose it to than Linda Street?*

✦ ✦ ✦

Prom night was the only time Linda and Jerry had sex. They dated for the rest of Linda's senior year and through the summer. They made out occasionally, but it never led further. Jerry would have been willing if Linda had wanted to, but he was just as glad she didn't. He was still feeling guilty. Instead, they became great friends.

It was a sad day when Linda went off to college. They hugged for a long time.

That same year, the Streets moved to California. Linda's dad had been promoted into a big job. Linda wrote a few times, and Jerry always wrote back, but soon the letters stopped coming. He wrote her a few more times but received no response. The final letter came back marked, **Return to Sender**.

PART ONE

1

November 23, thirty-two days before Christmas

The fire in the fireplace of Joseph Fleet's study gave off a warm glow, remindful of the holiday season and the events of the night. Another Fleet Thanksgiving extravaganza was in the books, and Joseph Fleet and I were having our annual after-dinner drinks.

"You're looking well," I said.

A few years ago, when we shared our traditional drink, Joseph Fleet had told me he had an inoperable brain tumor. The prognosis had not been good. So far, he was beating the odds.

"I'm well most of the time," he said. "Headaches now and then. The treatment has shrunk the tumor some, but now it seems at a standstill, not getting smaller or bigger. I'm living life one day at a time and enjoying every minute."

"That's good to hear, sir," I said. "We'd like to keep you around for a while."

"You've had an interesting year," he said. "The Gildersleeve case, the golf tournaments, and a sniper attack. Whatever happened with that? What have you been doing lately?"

"The sniper is out of the picture," I said. "His past caught up with him. As for me, I pretty much took the summer off and stayed at the lake house. Mary and I went to Mexico for a couple of weeks to visit Henry and Rosa. I went into the office every now and then just to show my face. I helped out on a few FBI cases as a consultant, but they weren't very exciting. I promised Mary I'd try to avoid danger-ous situations. Thankfully, I haven't found any on my doorstep."

"I think you've had enough dangerous situations to last a couple of lifetimes," Joseph Fleet said. "I'm happy to hear you're staying out of harm's way."

"Thank you, sir," I said, raising my glass and taking a drink of Baileys Irish Cream. Joseph Fleet had tried many times to get me to quit calling him "sir," but I couldn't do it. Our relationship had started when he hired me to find his missing daughter. Calling him "sir" just came naturally.

"I hear that you're on the board of Durbinfield Financial," Joseph Fleet said.

I smiled. News traveled fast among the rich. "Yes, sir. Elizabeth is hard to say no to. She really didn't leave me much choice and made it quite clear that Lacy is going to be heir to a sizable fortune. My being on the board should be beneficial to Lacy in the future."

"Makes sense," Joseph Fleet said.

"What makes sense?" Mary said, standing in the doorway looking gorgeous as ever.

"My being hopelessly in love with you," I said.

I think Mary actually blushed. For a moment, she was flustered, speechless.

"Wow," she said. "That's the best thing I've heard since you said you'd marry me, you silver-tongued devil."

Joseph Fleet laughed as he stood up.

"Time to go, Cowboy," Mary said.

I got to my feet and turned to Joseph Fleet. I extended my hand. "Same time next year?"

"Same time, Donald," he said. "But don't be a stranger."

2

November 27, twenty-eight days before Christmas

The weekend after Thanksgiving was uneventful. Mary and I spent it at the lake house. Lacy, our adopted daughter, and her fiancé, Biker, stayed until Sunday. We drove them to the airport Sunday morning to catch a flight back to Arizona State, where they both attended college. They promised to be back for Christmas.

On Monday morning, I sat in my office staring out the window at snow flurries. I hadn't come to the office much in the last six months, and there was general surprise from Gretchen and Rhonda when I did. The first day of December was cold, with promises it would get even colder. Unfortunately, no significant snow was in the forecast, but the cold temperature meant the ski resorts in North Carolina would be making snow. That made me happy. I heard the outer office door open and close, and seconds later Gretchen stood in my doorway.

"You're in," she said, obviously surprised.

"I am."

"Stay put," she said. "I need to catch you up on some things."

"I'll be right here."

Minutes later, Gretchen was back. "Our workload is adequate," she said. "We're paying the bills and making a profit. The Cherokee office is another story. Billy doesn't charge enough."

Billy was Billy Two-Feathers, my best friend in college, a full-blooded Cherokee Indian, and my original partner—hence, Cherokee Investigations.

"It's a poor community," I said. "I'll be happy if the Cherokee office breaks even."

"Billy said he's working on something big that might cover his overhead for a year," Gretchen said. "He wouldn't elaborate."

"If Billy said even that much, then it must be promising," I said.

"I agree," Gretchen said. "So, for now, I'll leave Billy alone."

"Give him a year to get things going, and then we'll reassess," I said.

Billy had recently reopened the Cherokee office after a stint as a Swain County deputy sheriff. He had originally started with me in Mountain Center. We were still partners.

Gretchen nodded.

"What else?" I said.

"You need to be in the office more," Gretchen said. "When new clients come in, they like to know the big cheese is here, if only to meet him and say hello. You've had enough time off."

Knowing Gretchen, she had run this conversation starter by Mary, and Mary had told her to go for it.

"What do you have in mind?"

"Two or three days a week, and be on call if I need you to make an appearance."

"Agreed," I said. "How about I come in Mondays, Tuesdays, and Thursdays? If you need me for an appointment on Wednesday or Friday, I'll do it, but try to avoid those days."

"Agreed," Gretchen said. "Starting after the first of the year. I think things will be pretty slow in December."

"Deal," I said.

She got up to leave.

"Thanks for running a tight ship," I said. "I mean it. I need you to keep me focused sometimes."

"Honestly," Gretchen said, "with all you've been through, I think you're pretty amazing."

She turned and went back to her office before I could come up with a smart remark. Just as well. I had none.

✦ ✦ ✦

Midmorning, I called David Steele, deputy director of the FBI, whom I worked for from time to time as a special consultant.

"I'm bored out of my skull," I said. "Have you got anything I can work on?"

"Maybe," he said. "But it will be after the first of the year, and you'd have to go undercover."

"How long?"

"Don't know," he said. "As long as it takes. Mary could be part of it, if you could arrange it."

"Can you give me a clue?"

"Small-town corruption in the Deep South," he said.

"Interesting. Why is the FBI interested in small-town corruption in the Deep South?"

"Normally, we wouldn't be," he said. "But there's a twist. We'll talk more about it after New Year's."

✦ ✦ ✦

Later that afternoon, I called Roy Husky. I had to go through his assistant. I didn't like to call his cell phone during business hours unless it was an emergency.

"Are we on for tonight?" I said when he came on the line.

"Six o'clock," he said. "See you there."

✦ ✦ ✦

Mary and her girl gang, the Annie Oakleys, were having a ladies' night out, which usually meant I met Roy at the Bloody Duck, a blue-collar biker pool hall/bar and grill outside of town. The place could be a little rowdy but was mostly calm during the week. Rocky, the owner, was an old friend of Roy's, and we generally got special treatment, such as the back booth, away from the fray.

When we got there, the back booth was occupied.

"Have a drink at the bar," Rocky said. "I'll hustle these guys along."

The bar wasn't crowded. We took a spot and ordered a draft. I noticed a younger man a few spots down. He looked a little out of place. He was blond and good looking, with a neatly trimmed beard. He turned and smiled at me, and I was caught off guard by the most unusual blue eyes I had ever seen. I nodded and turned away. Then I heard an argument begin between two rough-looking bikers.

"It's my turn," one said.

"It is not," the other said, slightly louder.

"It is, too, asshole," came the retort, louder still.

"Who are you calling an asshole, dickweed?"

"You!"

"How would you like me to punch your lights out?"

"Take you best shot, pussy."

At this point, Rocky pulled what looked like a miniature baseball bat from under the bar and started for the two combatants. Before he could get there, the good-looking blond guy came off his barstool, stepped between the two brutes, and put a hand on each one's chest.

"Gentlemen," he said calmly, "it's the holiday season. Let's show some goodwill."

The bar became deathly quiet as the two bikers looked with surprise at the blond guy. Rocky stopped to watch. I waited for the blond guy to get creamed. It didn't happen. The bikers looked at one another, then back to the blond guy.

"You're right, it's nothing to fight about," the bigger of the two said. "You go ahead," he said to the other biker.

"That's okay, you go ahead," the other one said. "I think it's your turn."

"Thanks," the first one said.

Just like that, it was over, and the blond guy returned to his beer. Rocky put away his club, looked up at us, and smiled.

"Your booth is ready," he said.

For reasons I still cannot fathom, I heard myself say to the blond guy, "Would you like to join us for a burger and fries? My treat."

The blond man looked at Roy.

"Join us," Roy said.

"It would be my pleasure," the blond man said.

We walked to the back booth. I sat beside Roy, and the blond guy sat across from us.

"I'm Don Youngblood, and he's Roy Husky," I said.

"Jeremiah James," he said. "Pleased to meet you."

"That was pretty brave, what you did back there," Roy said. "It could have gone wrong."

"I sometimes act before I think," Jeremiah said. "I guess someone is looking out for me."

A waitress came by and took our order. Jeremiah seemed relaxed, confident, and comfortable in the company of two strangers. I guessed his age to be mid-thirties to early forties, but he could have been older. The older I got, the harder it was for me to judge age.

"Brave is what you did at the PGA Championship," he said. "I'm a big golf fan. I was watching. You saved a lot of lives."

"There's probably someone looking out for me, too," I said.

Jeremiah smiled. "I'm sure there is."

"Where are you from?" Roy asked, steering away from a subject he knew I didn't wish to talk about.

"I was born in North Carolina," Jeremiah said. "Small town."

"What do you do for a living?" Roy asked.

"Traveling handyman. I do electrical, plumbing, painting, but mostly carpentry, inside and outside."

"How long will you be in Mountain Center?" I said.

"Don't know," he said. "Depends on if I can find work and a place to stay. I hope I can stay until after New Year's."

"So, you move around a lot," Roy said.

We were doing pretty well with the double-team third degree. He seemed not to mind.

"Yes," Jeremiah said. "I'm sort of a nomad. I wander. I pick a town, meet people, work, and when I get the feeling it's time to go, I go. Sometimes it's a month, other times three months, and other times a lot longer."

Our food arrived with another round of draft beer.

"How long have you been doing this?" Roy said.

"Long time," Jeremiah said.

"No family?" I said.

"None," he said.

So ended the interrogation. We turned our attention to our food and lighter conversation. There was something about Jeremiah that I couldn't quite grasp. Nothing sinister, I was sure. Mysterious, maybe. A relatively young, good-looking guy wandering around the country. I sensed an interesting back-story, one that he wasn't going to share.

By the time we finished dinner, I had an idea. "I might know a place you could stay for a while," I said. "A pretty nice trailer park not far from here. I can make a call, if you're interested."

"Sounds good," Jeremiah said. "How much, do you think?"

"I know the manager," I said. "I'll work something out you can afford."

I barely knew the manager. I didn't even know his full name. Everyone called him Rizzo. Rizzo was an ass-hole. I had a run-in with him during the Three Devils case. He was uncooperative until Big Bob Wilson, my best friend in high school and the current Mountain Center chief of police, had chewed him out. Then he couldn't do enough for me. I made the call.

"Mountain Center Trailer Park," he answered. "This is Rizzo."

"Rizzo, this is Donald Youngblood. Remember me?"

"Sure, Mr. Youngblood," he said, friendly as could be. "Private cop, friend of the chief. Am I in trouble?"

"No, Rizzo, you're not in trouble. I need a favor."

"If I can do it, you got it," he said. *Mr. Helpful.*

"I have a friend who needs a place for a month or two," I said. "I was wondering if you have any trailers for rent."

"You're in luck," he said. "One just became available. A nice one. Fully furnished."

"How much?"

He paused. "One person?"

"Yes. One very nice young man. His name is Jeremiah."

"Okay. For you, I could do five hundred a month. And that's a deal, let me tell you."

"Thanks, Rizzo," I said. "I owe you one. He'll be there in about an hour." I looked at Jeremiah for confirmation, and he nodded.

"That's fine," Rizzo said. "It's clean and ready. How will I get paid?"

"Call my office tomorrow," I said.

"Will do," he said. "If I ever need a private cop, you're it."

"I'm flattered. Goodbye, Rizzo."

Before we left, Jeremiah and I exchanged cell-phone numbers.

"Call me if you need anything," I said. "I'll spread the word that you're looking for work."

"Thank you," Jeremiah said. "You've been very kind."

" 'Tis the season," I said.

"Indeed it is," he said.

✦ ✦ ✦

"How was your dinner?" I asked Mary later that night at our downtown condo.

"Fun," she said. "A laugh a minute."

"How many showed up?"

"Gretchen, Rhonda, Jerri, Wanda, Estelle, Sylvia, Susie, and me."

"You're expanding."

"We are," Mary said.

"Estelle has a gun carry permit?" I said. A gun carry permit was required to join the Annie Oakleys.

"Much to my surprise," Mary said.

Estelle was Rollie Ogle's assistant, a sweet, savvy, attractive older woman who seemed as gentle as a summer breeze. Rollie was a divorce lawyer who had an office on the same floor I did. He frequently used Cherokee Investigations to gather information on wayward husbands.

"Any interesting news?"

"Not really," Mary said. "How was your night out with Roy?"

"Very interesting."

Mary was immediately curious. "Tell me all," she said.

So I did.

"What prompted you to ask him to join you and then help him find a place to stay?"

"I don't know," I said. "It just came out of my mouth before I could stop it. There's something unusual about this young guy."

"You'll figure it out," Mary said. "You always do. I'm getting ready for bed."

✦ ✦ ✦

Later, in bed, Mary said, "You know, I'll bet the dock and boathouse could use some work."

"Not a bad idea. Let me give that some thought."

Mary turned out the light and scooted close to me so we could spoon. "Good night, my love," she said.

I kissed her neck. "Goodnight, Mrs. Youngblood," I said, and held her tight.

3

November 28, twenty-seven days before Christmas

The next morning, on a whim, I took the dogs to the office. Midmorning, the office phone rang, and then my intercom buzzed.

"Some guy named Rizzo is on line one," Gretchen said. "Sounds like he's from Jersey."

"Rizzo," I said. "What's up?"

"Your guy is in the trailer," he said. "You were right. Nice guy."

Surprisingly, Rizzo sounded different, sincere even.

"I'll send you a check for a thousand today," I said. "Unless you want to stop by and get it."

"No hurry. Glad I could help. Happy holidays."

"And you," I said. "Goodbye, Rizzo."

I smiled to myself. Rizzo actually sounded like a real human being. *Must be the season*, I thought.

✦ ✦ ✦

Later that morning, I heard the outer office door open and close. Muted voices I couldn't quite understand came from the other side of my closed door. My intercom buzzed.

"Jeremiah James to see you," Gretchen said.

"Show him in, please," I said. *Politeness is all.*

Jeremiah came in, and I motioned him to one of the oversized chairs in front of my desk. The dogs came over to sniff him. He knelt to pet them, first Junior, then Jake. He gave Jake a good rub and a final pat and stood up.

"Nice dogs," he said.

"Thanks," I said. "Sit a minute."

"That's all right," he said, still standing. "I can't stay. I just came by to thank you for helping me get settled."

"You're welcome. Glad I could help."

"I've been going around introducing myself to some of the shopkeepers," he said. "I've got a few odd jobs already."

"That was quick," I said. "Why don't you let me take you to a late breakfast and introduce you to the owner of the Mountain Center Diner? She'll be a good person to help spread the word."

"You're very kind, Mr. Youngblood," Jeremiah said.

✦ ✦ ✦

We slipped through the back door of the diner and sat at the table Doris always kept open for me. It didn't take her long to spot us. She came over with a puzzled look, having noted an unfamiliar face at my table.

When she arrived, I said, "Doris, meet Jeremiah James. Jeremiah is new in town. Jeremiah, this is Doris Black, owner of this fine establishment."

Jeremiah stood and with a slight nod said, "It's a pleasure to meet you, Doris."

Doris beamed. "Well, thank you. It's a pleasure to meet you, too, Jeremiah. What can I get you-all?"

"The usual," I said.

"I'll have what he's having," Jeremiah said.

"Feta cheese omelet, home fries, rye toast, and coffee," Doris said, looking at Jeremiah for conformation.

"Perfect," he said.

Doris hurried away and returned with coffee before a minute elapsed.

"Where were you last?" I said.

Jeremiah smiled. "A town in Kentucky, Clay. Nice little town. How long have you been a private investigator?"

"Over ten years," I said.

"I like what I've seen of Mountain Center. And I seem to have had the good fortune of meeting the most famous person in town."

"Ah, you have a laptop, I take it."

"I do," he said. "I confess I researched you. You've had an interesting life."

"That's true," I said. "Did I mention that I hate the Internet?"

"As do I most of the time," he said.

Our food arrived, and we got down to the business of eating. Jeremiah asked a lot of questions about Mountain Center: where were the lumberyard, the hardware store, the electrical supply, and, surprisingly, the local Methodist church? When we were finished, Doris cleared our plates, and I told her to spread the word we had a new handyman in town. She was more than happy to do so.

Walking back to the office, I said, "I have a bigger job, if you're interested. I live part-time on a lake and have a boathouse and dock that probably could use some refurbishing."

"I'd prefer a big job," Jeremiah said. "When can I take a look?"

"Tomorrow morning okay?"

"Sure," he said. "What's the address?"

I told him, and he wrote it down in a small notebook. At the back door leading up to my office, he said goodbye, then surprised me again when he walked over to a nearby Harley, fired it up, and rode away. I watched him go, wanting more and more to know his story.

✦ ✦ ✦

Back in the office, Gretchen said, "Who was that hunk you went to breakfast with?"

"That's Jeremiah James," I said. "About all I know are his name and that he's new in town."

"Really good looking," Gretchen said. "And those eyes."

"Down, girl," I said. "You already have a good-looking blond guy."

Gretchen's main squeeze was FBI agent Buckley Clarke, who worked out of the Knoxville office. Buckley spent a lot of time in Mountain Center.

"True," Gretchen said. "But a girl can look."

4

November 29, twenty-six days before Christmas

The following morning, I drove out to the lake house to meet Jeremiah James. His Harley was parked in the driveway, but there was no sign of him. I unlocked the front door and went down the hall to the kitchen and out the back door onto the upper deck. Jeremiah was on the dock getting a good look at what repairs should be done. He saw me and waved.

"Want coffee?" I shouted.

"That would be nice!" he shouted back. "I'll be up in a minute."

I went back into the house and brewed a pot, using my Mr. Coffee. While it was brewing, I went back outside and shouted, "How do you take it?"

"Black!" he shouted back.

I went inside and poured coffee into two Yeti insulated mugs, fixed mine the way I liked it, and went back outside. I walked down to the lower deck as Jeremiah was coming up the stairs from the dock.

"Nice day," he said.

The temperature had risen into the fifties and the sun was out, a pleasant day for December. East Tennessee had a way of offering a variety of weather in a short period of time.

"It is," I said, handing him the Yeti with the black coffee.

We sat at the table where earlier in the year a sniper's bullet had almost removed me from planet earth. The scar left by one of the bullets on the umbrella post reminded me of how lucky I was. It was also a reminder of how dangerous my line of work could be.

"What do you think?" I said.

"It could use some repairs," he said. "There's some dry rot that will only get worse, and the beginning of some more dry rot that I can sand out. I'll need some new lumber, screws, and paint. When I'm finished, it will look brand-new."

"Let's do it," I said. "When can you start?"

"It's supposed to rain or snow for the next couple of days," he said. "And I've volunteered to do some maintenance at Mountain Center Methodist Church. So, why don't I start on Monday? Next week is going to be milder, and there's no rain in the forecast."

"Sounds like a plan," I said. "I have an account at the hardware store, so charge anything you need. I'll let the owner know. Purchase the best possible stuff. If I'm going to do this, I want it done right."

"Good to hear," Jeremiah said. "Thanks for the coffee. I have to run. I have a couple of more odd jobs to do."

He went down the steps to the side yard and up toward the driveway. Moments later, I heard the Harley engine rev. The sound faded until I heard his engine as he turned onto the main road and pulled away toward Mountain Center. Soon, I heard nothing. *This guy is too good to be true*, I thought.

✦ ✦ ✦

That night, Mary and I were having drinks at the kitchen bar in our downtown condo.

"Jeremiah James agreed to do the boathouse and deck work," I said. "That was a good idea on your part."

"I look forward to meeting him," Mary said. "I hear he's a hunk."

"You've been talking to Gretchen."

Mary smiled and said nothing. We drank some wine and were quiet for a while.

"I want to go to church on Sunday," I said.

We went to church maybe once a month, if that, but I always enjoyed the early contemporary service.

"I can't believe it," Mary said. "I was thinking the same thing. Isn't that strange?"

Maybe not, I thought.

5

December 3, twenty-two days before Christmas

Mountain Center Methodist was by far the largest church in town. That was unusual, given the fact that the Southern Baptists ruled our region. The church had four services, two at eight-thirty and two at eleven. One service in each time slot was contemporary.

Mary and I arrived early and secured aisle seats. A few people we knew stopped by to say hello. The senior minister, Adam Church, was doing the service today. Adam usually preached at the eleven o'clock traditional service. He stopped by our seats and greeted us.

"So good to see you two," he said. "Welcome. Don, hang around after the service if you can. I'd like to talk to you." Adam moved away.

"Know what that's about?" Mary said.

"I think so," I said. Music started to play. The service was beginning. "I'll tell you about it later."

The service lifted my spirits, as did the signs of Christmas sprinkled throughout the fellowship hall, where the contemporary service was held. I estimated one hundred and fifty people in attendance. They strolled from the fellowship hall after the service, some greeting Adam and others not taking the time. I waited. When the last person had gone, Adam walked over.

"Thanks for waiting," he said. "I have a question."

"About Jeremiah James, I'll bet."

"Yes. How did you know?"

"Jeremiah told me he was doing some volunteer work here," I said.

"He seems like a nice young man. And so far, he has done excellent work and made some good suggestions. He is certainly well educated in theology. We've had some interesting discussions. What do you know about him?"

"Not much," I said. "We met at the Bloody Duck."

"The Bloody Duck?"

"You haven't heard of it?"

"Afraid not," he said.

"It's not as bad as it sounds," I said. "I know the owner and go out there occasionally with a friend.

They make the best burgers around." I told him about the night I met Jeremiah and the events that followed.

"He does have a real mature, calming presence about him," Adam said. "He wants to do a live Nativity in front of the church. He said if I sanction it, he'll organize it and build the stable and manger."

"And what did you say?"

"I said I'd discuss it with the staff and some key church members and let him know," Adam said. "The more I think about the live Nativity, the more I like the idea. I wanted your input."

"I can't think of any reason for you to say no," I said.

"Indeed," Adam said. "Well, thanks for your time. I was just curious about Jeremiah. I get a little nosy sometimes."

"I know that feeling," I said.

6

December 4, twenty-one days before Christmas

After church, Mary and I went to the lake house. Later in the day, I cleared out the boathouse and tied off the barge at the end of the dock in preparation for Jeremiah's visit.

Monday morning, a white van drove down our driveway and parked off to the side, so as not to block either of us from leaving. Jeremiah went around the side yard to the back of the house and started setting up. I walked out on the back deck. Jeremiah was at the bottom of the stairs that led to the deck. The deck ran across the yard at water's edge. A section in the center ran straight out into the lake, forming a giant inverted *T*.

"Coffee?"

"Sure," he said.

"Come up to the kitchen. I'd like you to meet my wife."

"Give me a couple of minutes," he said.

When Jeremiah came in, I poured him a mug of coffee and one for myself. Moments later, Mary entered the kitchen looking gorgeous as ever in dark gray slacks, white blouse, black leather jacket, black boots, badge on her belt, and gun on her hip. *Be still my heart.*

She didn't wait for introductions. "Jeremiah," she said, "I'm Mary Youngblood, his better half."

"Obviously," he said. "Very pleased to meet you."

"I like him already," Mary said to me. "I have to run. Pleasure meeting you, Jeremiah."

"Thank you," Jeremiah said.

"I'll see you tonight at the condo," she said, and kissed me goodbye.

"Your wife seems nice," Jeremiah said after Mary closed the front door.

"One in a million," I said. "I'm going to the office. Call me if you need anything. Want me to leave the house open?"

"No," he said. "Lock up. I have everything I need."

✦ ✦ ✦

Later that morning, Adam Church called.

"I wanted to let you know that we decided to do the live Nativity, and I wanted to let Jeremiah know," he said. "Trouble is, I don't know how to get in touch with him. We're going to have a meeting Wednesday night to discuss the particulars, and I want him to be there."

"Jeremiah is doing some work for me this week," I said. "I'll be sure he knows about your meeting and suggest that he call you."

"Thank you so much, Don," Adam Church said.

I called Jeremiah and gave him the news.

"That's great," he said. "I'll call Pastor Church as soon as I finish my day here."

7

December 6, nineteen days before Christmas

Wednesday, I drove to the lake house at lunchtime with sandwiches and chips I picked up at Carrie Lee's Diner. I had called Jeremiah and told him I was coming. He seemed pleased. I sat on the lower deck and watched him work for a few minutes. He was using a power sander, and I wasn't sure whether or not he'd seen me. The boathouse and deck were a patchwork of new wood, sanded wood, and sound old wood. Jeremiah stopped the sander and looked toward me. I waved him up. He put the sander down and came to the lower deck.

"Diet Coke, club sandwich, and chips," I said.

"Great," he said. "I'm hungry."

We unwrapped the sandwiches, popped open the Diet Cokes, and tore open the chips. We used paper plates to hold our lunches.

"Do you mind if I pray?" Jeremiah said.

"Not at all," I said.

"Dear Father in heaven," he began. "Thank you so much for Don, who has provided this meal today. Thank you for all your blessings and all that you do for us. Bless this fellowship as we spend time sharing this meal. In the name of the Father, the Son, and the Holy Spirit, amen."

"Amen," I echoed.

We began to eat.

"How's it going out there?"

"I'm finished with the board replacement. I have more sanding to do. I should be ready to start painting tomorrow."

"It appears you're doing a fine job," I said.

"Thank you," Jeremiah said. "I love jobs like this. It gives me a real sense of accomplishment when I'm finished." He took a bite of his sandwich.

"How's the trailer working out?"

"Fine," he said. "The manager has been very attentive. He either likes you a lot or he's afraid of you."

"I don't think he likes me even a little. He's afraid of the chief of police, who's a good friend of mine."

"I see," Jeremiah said.

We were silent for a while, concentrating on our lunches.

"How did you learn carpentry?"

"I worked for a builder when I was in college," he said. "I helped build two houses one summer. He taught me a lot. I hated to leave him."

I took a big bite of my sandwich and ate some chips. I didn't want to ask too many questions, figuring that sooner or later he would ask me one. I waited.

"Why did you choose to be a private investigator?"

"I was on Wall Street making lots of money, but I was lonely and bored. One day, I decided to pack up and come home. Billy Two-Feathers, my best friend in college, came with me. I opened Cherokee Investigations because I thought it would be interesting work and because Mountain Center didn't have a private investigator. Billy got work as a forensic photographer, and I got a few small cases. I wasn't very motivated because I didn't need the money. Then I got a big case and ended up working with another college friend who was in the FBI. After that, big cases started falling into my lap. Now, I cannot imagine doing anything else."

"It sounds like the job chose you," Jeremiah said.

"Feels like it, too," I said.

We were silent for a while.

"Don't you get lonely roaming from town to town?"

"No," he said. "It's my way of life. It's what I do. I enjoy meeting new people. Bad people get all the attention, and the good people for the most part go unnoticed. Most people are good. They keep me going." He finished his Diet Coke, set the can down, and got up. "Got to get back to it. Not a lot of daylight this time of year." He went back down the stairs to the dock.

I cleaned up and went inside. I was about to throw everything in the trash when, on an impulse, I held out Jeremiah's Diet Coke can. I slipped it into a Ziploc bag and took it with me, feeling guilty as I did. I walked past his van, stopped, and looked inside. There were lots of tools. They looked used but in excellent condition. The van was immaculate. *Who is this man*? I thought.

✦ ✦ ✦

Back in the office, I called Scott Glass, longtime friend and FBI agent in charge of the Salt Lake City office. We had worked a few cases together. I could usually count on him for off-the-record stuff.

"Professor," I said when he came on the phone, "how have you been?"

"Well, if it isn't the famous Donald Youngblood. How are you, Blood, and what do you want? I know this isn't a social call."

"Cynical as always," I said.

"And with good reason," he said. "Spill it."

"I have a Diet Coke can with a set of prints on it. I need to put a name and some background with those prints."

"What's this about, Blood?"

"I'm not really sure, Professor. You'll have to trust me on this one. It may be nothing. In fact, I hope it's nothing. But I need to check."

"Well, given your track record, it will probably be something. Send me the can. I'll give it to John, and he'll get back to you."

"Let's keep this between you, me, and John," I said.

"We can do that."

"I owe you one, Scott," I said.

"Right," he said.

I thought he sounded rather sarcastic. *The FBI!*

✦ ✦ ✦

Later, I gave Gretchen the can. "Pack this up and send it overnight to Scott Glass."

Gretchen looked curiously at the can and then at me, waiting for an explanation.

"This is between you and me," I said. "Understand?"

"Understood," she said. "I'll get it out today."

8

December 7, eighteen days before Christmas

The next day, I again took lunch to Jeremiah. Maybe I felt guilty. He said grace, and we started to eat.

"You're going to spoil me," he said.

"I was curious to see how you're doing," I said. "I promise not to bring lunch tomorrow."

The painting on the deck appeared to be about half finished. The boathouse was completely finished, and I had to admit it looked brand-new.

"It's coming along," he said.

"It looks terrific. Will you finish tomorrow?"

"Yes," Jeremiah said. "Tomorrow for sure."

✦ ✦ ✦

Late that afternoon, Big Bob Wilson dropped by. The Mountain Center chief of police rarely visited my office in the afternoon. He occasionally came by for coffee in the morning.

"Anybody with him?" I heard him say.

"He's alone," Gretchen said.

The big man didn't wait to be announced. He just barged right in. Protocol was not high on his list of priorities.

"The coffee is long gone," I said.

"I didn't come for coffee. Who the hell is Jeremiah James? Half the town has asked me if I've met him. Supposedly, he's a friend of yours."

"He's a handyman I met a few days ago at the Bloody Duck when he broke up a potential fight. He's done some odd jobs around town, and now he's refurbishing my deck and boathouse."

"Everyone seems to think he's wonderful," Big Bob said. "Do you know anything about him?"

"Not much. He seems like a nice-enough guy. Why do you care?"

"Because I'm the chief of police, and I'm paid to care. Does he do good work?"

"Seems to," I said. "Did you get any complaints?"

"No," the big man said. "Everybody seems happy with his work. I also heard he volunteered free labor at Mountain Center Methodist Church."

I smiled. "Nothing gets by you."

"Are you the least bit suspicious?"

"Curious, maybe," I said.

"Going to do anything about that curiosity?"

"I might."

"Let me know if you find out anything I should know," he said.

"Will do."

He blew out of my office like a big wind.

9

December 8, seventeen days before Christmas

By the time I got to the lake house Friday afternoon, the deck was finished and Jeremiah was gone. A note and a bill for the work were taped to the front door. The bill was very reasonable. The note said,

Stay off the deck for 24 hours. Blessings, Jeremiah.

His handwriting was unusual and artistic.

✦ ✦ ✦

Midafternoon on Saturday, Mary and I walked on the deck and inspected Jeremiah's work.

"It's flawless," Mary said. "It's like brand-new. You have to be pleased."

"I am. This guy is too good to be true."

"Funny," Mary said, "I was thinking the same thing. Why is that?"

"We're being influenced by the line of work we're in. We're paid to be suspicious."

"Well, I hope we don't have anything to be suspicious about," Mary said.

"So do I."

I moved the houseboat from the end of the barge into the boathouse and tied it up. The inside of the boathouse was as flawless as the outside.

✦ ✦ ✦

Sunday, we again went to church. Two in a row—a personal record for us.

"I'd like to go church again," Mary had said in the kitchen when we were having coffee.

"Me, too," I said.

Pastor Adam Church was doing the traditional later service, so that's the one we attended. I enjoyed his message. I noticed an announcement in the bulletin about the live Nativity.

As we were making our way out of the sanctuary, Jeremiah James spotted us and came over to say hello. "It's nice to see you two," he said. "I heard you were here last Sunday also."

"I guess you're a good influence," Mary said.

"I certainly hope so," Jeremiah said.

I said nothing.

Jeremiah nodded and walked away to speak with other attendees. Pastor Adam came over to greet us.

"How did your Nativity meeting go?" I said.

"Wonderful," Adam said. "Everyone is excited. We decided on the three nights right before Christmas."

10

December 10, fifteen days before Christmas

John Banks called me Monday afternoon on my
cell.

"Nothing off the prints on the can," he said.
"They're not in any criminal database that I have
access to, and I have access to a lot. They could be in
some local database, but you'd need to steer me in the
right direction. It would be helpful to have a name."

"Jeremiah James," I said. "Try birth records in
North Carolina."

"Okay," John said. "That helps. I'll be in touch."

✦ ✦ ✦

Things were slow at the office and I was about to fall
asleep in my chair when I decided to take a drive over
to Mountain Center Methodist. The church sat on a
large tract of land and was beautifully landscaped. It
had a full-time custodian who always seemed to be
busy painting something, trimming something, or
mowing something. The large grassy area to the left
of the main entrance was piled with new lumber—
not much doubt that it would be used to build the
Nativity. Jeremiah was nowhere in sight.

I didn't feel much like going back to the office, so I drove to the condo. As I was walking through the front door, John Banks called.

"The only Jeremiah James I found in the North Carolina birth records was born in 1944 in Franklin," he said. "I would have thought there'd be more, but there wasn't. Can that be your guy?"

"No," I said. "My guy is much younger."

"Anything else I can do?"

"Not right now, John. Thanks. I'll be in touch if I need you."

✦ ✦ ✦

That night at the kitchen bar sharing a bottle of pre-dinner wine, I told Mary my plans for the next day.

"That really is a long shot," she said. "Why do you have to know?"

"Better to know than not to know."

"You're becoming obsessed."

"Maybe," I said, "but it does give me something to do."

"I've got something you can do," Mary said.

"What's that?"

"I'll give you a hint."

She came off her barstool, put one hand behind my head, and pulled me toward her. She kissed me passionately. I kissed her back.

"Oh, that," I said.

"That," Mary said.

Dinner was a long time waiting.

11

December 11, fourteen days before Christmas

The following day, I drove south to Franklin, North Carolina. There was snow in the mountains, but the roads were clear. On my way, I thought about the best place to start my quest. I decided on the local Methodist church. I found the church, found the office, and asked the administrative assistant if the senior pastor was in. He was, and he agreed to see me. Pastor Joe Greene was a stocky older man with short-cut gray hair and a pleasant face. I introduced myself.

"What can I do for you, Mr. Youngblood?" he said.

"I'm a private investigator from Mountain Center, Tennessee, trying to track down a family member for a relative," I said. It wasn't the first little white lie I had told a minister—better than having to explain my obsession. I handed him my card. He took a long look and then looked back at me.

"The PGA tournament, right?" he said. "You're him."

"Yes," I said.

"Courageous thing you did. I couldn't believe my eyes."

"Thank you. I've been trying to put it behind me."

"I understand," he said. "Now, how can I help you?"

"I'm trying to locate a man named Jeremiah James, born here in 1944. I wondered if you might know if he's still around, or if you know someone who might know."

"I wouldn't know," he said. "I haven't been here that long. The Methodist Church usually doesn't let us stay more than six years at any one church. I've been here three years. This is my last stop before retirement."

"Who would know the most about town history?" I said.

"Oh, that would be Miss Maples. She's a member here, a retired librarian. I could call her. She loves company."

"That would be great," I said.

He made the call, and Miss Maples agreed to see me. According to Pastor Greene, she was excited. He gave me directions and an address. I thanked him for his time and left.

✦ ✦ ✦

Miss Maples lived on a quiet street not far from the center of town. I was there within ten minutes. She lived in an older house, but it looked well cared for.

"Come in, come in, Mr. Youngblood." she said excitedly as she opened the door. "I made coffee. I hope you'll have some."

She obviously knew who I was. We skipped introductions.

"Sure," I said. "Coffee sounds good."

"Come into the kitchen, and we'll sit at the table."

I followed her into the kitchen. The house was spotless and filled with antiques. I wondered how old she was. We sat, and she poured coffee. Cream and sugar were on the table, and we both used them. She was an attractive little white-haired woman who seemed as well cared for as the house.

"That's real cream," she said.

"Bless you," I said.

She laughed.

I fixed my coffee the way I wanted it and took a sip. Excellent.

"I have a microwave, if it cools off too much," she said.

I nodded and took another sip. "Nice house."

"Old," she said. "Like me."

"You and the house both seem to be holding up well," I said.

"Thank you. Not bad for ninety."

"I would have never guessed it," I said, and I meant it. She didn't look her age.

"Thank you. Now, tell me, Mr. Youngblood, what can I do for you?"

"Please call me Don or Donald," I said. "I answer to both. I wondered if you knew a Jeremiah James. Supposedly, he was born here in 1944."

"Well, I didn't know him personally. I think I must have been about twelve or thirteen when Jeremiah was born. His father was a Methodist minister at our church. Same church where you met Reverend Greene."

Now I was getting somewhere. "Did Jeremiah have any children?"

"Oh, no," she said. "Jeremiah died in a rock-climbing accident out west in the early sixties. And then there was that horrible mess about his body."

"What horrible mess?"

"First, they couldn't find his body. They said it got misplaced in the morgue. Then they told the local chief of police it had been cremated by mistake. So, they sent the ashes. How are you supposed to know it's the right ashes? Anyway, the town held a memorial ceremony at the football stadium and spread the ashes on the field. He was quite the athlete, you know."

"No way to know if they were really his ashes," I said.

"You are so right. Such a tragedy. You see, he had no family. His mother and father were killed in a horrible car wreck in Atlanta in Jeremiah's senior year. He had no aunts or uncles, brothers or sisters, nobody. He had just turned eighteen. What a nice boy. Handsome. Blond hair and the most beautiful blue eyes. What a waste. So sad. I guess I'm rambling a bit."

I was reeling from this latest piece of news. She was describing the Jeremiah I knew, but it couldn't be the same person. Sometime in his young life, the older Jeremiah had found time to father a child.

"Do you remember where the accident occurred?"

"Somewhere in New Mexico, I think," she said. "I'm pretty sure that's right."

"Anything else you can remember about him?"

"Well," she said, "he was kind of a hometown hero. As I said, good in sports, and a terrific artist. A mural he painted is still on the side of one of the old buildings downtown."

We talked longer. I knew she wanted me to stay awhile, so I did. Even at ninety, she was sharp and had some good stories to tell. I didn't learn anything else about Jeremiah James. She had told me all she remembered. I left in time to get home before dark.

✦ ✦ ✦

"It doesn't add up," Mary said.

We were having our usual drink before dinner. Pizza was in the oven keeping warm. The aroma filled the kitchen, causing our standard poodles, Jake and Junior, to be on high alert.

"I know," I said. "The Jeremiah born in 1944 died, let's say, in 1964. So, that would make him twenty at the time. If he fathered a child right before he died, the child would have to be in his late fifties right now."

"So, our Jeremiah would have to be a grandchild of the Jeremiah born in 1944."

"Seems so," I said.

"So, if our Jeremiah was born in North Carolina like he said, why doesn't he show up in the birth records?"

"Don't know," I said. "But you can bet I'm going to try and find out."

12

December 12, thirteen days before Christmas

Early Wednesday morning, I visited T. Elbert on his front porch. Roy was already there, and coffee and muffins were waiting. The day was a cold, overcast one, but the porch was warm from the overhead heaters that T. Elbert had installed years ago. I wondered what his heat bill was. I poured coffee, stirred in cream and sugar, and grabbed a corn muffin.

"Roy was telling me about Jeremiah the peacemaker at the Bloody Duck," T. Elbert said. "Wish I'd been there."

"I didn't think it was going to turn out well, but it did," I said. "Jeremiah has sure made himself known to a lot of people in a short time."

I caught them up on the adventures of Jeremiah James since that night at the Bloody Duck.

"He seems to have a positive effect on everyone he meets," T. Elbert said. "Even you, Donald. Church two Sundays in a row?"

" 'Tis the season," I said.

"And you're happy with his work," T. Elbert said.

"First rate. He takes his time and does it right."

"Only way to be," T. Elbert said.

"Has Mr. Fleet left for Amelia Island yet?" I said to Roy.

"Not yet," Roy said. "For some reason, he's waiting."

We talked awhile longer. I finished my coffee and muffin.

"I've got a meeting," Roy said. "See you next week."

I stayed a few minutes longer and then said good-bye. I was anxious to follow up on a thought I had while talking to Roy and T. Elbert.

✦ ✦ ✦

The only person I knew in New Mexico was a deputy sheriff I had dealings with while working the Clown case. His name was Danny West, a young Native American I was in a shootout with when I killed my first and only woman. She was a serial killer, rare for a woman, and I was not at all unhappy I had stopped her. Danny and I were both wounded and formed a special bond like soldiers in a war. I waited until midmorning to call him. It had been some time since I last talked to Danny.

"Youngblood," he said when he answered. "How are you, my friend?"

"I'm good, Danny. Still wearing those cool shades?"

He laughed. "Always," he said.

The first time I met Danny West, I had just come down the stairs from Fleet Industries jet number one to find a young deputy sheriff leaning against the right front fender of his SUV, sunglasses on, arms folded, blank expression on his face. Mr. Cool. The image made me smile.

"Danny, I need a favor."

"What do you need?"

"A young rock climber named Jeremiah James supposedly died in New Mexico in a climbing accident around 1964," I said. "I wonder if you could look into it and see if you can find anything—death certificate, newspaper articles, coroner's report, anything."

"Jeremiah James," he said. "Got it. You working a cold case?"

"I'm trying to solve a mystery. It's a real puzzle."

"I'll see what I can find," Danny said. "It may take a few days."

"Whatever you can do," I said. "I'll owe you one."

"You'll never owe me anything, Youngblood," he said. "You saved my ass, and I'll not forget it. I'll be in touch."

"Thanks, Danny," I said.

13

December 14, eleven days before Christmas

Thursday morning, I drove by Mountain Center Methodist Church before I went to the office. A work crew was out front with Pastor Church. I didn't see Jeremiah. I pulled into the parking lot and got out. Sections of the Nativity were scattered around the grounds in different stages of construction. Some were being nailed and others painted.

The good reverend walked over to where I stood watching. "We're making great progress," he said.

"I can see that," I said. "Where's Jeremiah?"

"He's putting a smaller Nativity in the main window of King's Department Store," Adam said.

"He does get around, doesn't he?"

"He does. And he seems to have positive effects everywhere he goes. He wanted to go to the hospital with me on a visitation yesterday. We visited an older parishioner who has pneumonia and was not expected to be with us much longer. Jeremiah prayed over her, and I'm telling you, I have never heard a more beautiful prayer. I called this morning to check on her, and she's much improved. The doctor thinks she's going to make it. How about that?"

"Power of prayer," I said.

"Indeed," Adam said. "And then Jeremiah went to the children's ward and visited. Read them Bible stories. They were very attentive. He's a special young man. I hope he settles here."

Not likely, I thought. "I hope so, too," I said.

"Jeremiah is building the Nativity so that we can take it down and reassemble it next year," Adam said. "He's also carving some life-sized figurines to use when we're not doing the live Nativity. We have some good artists in the church, and they're working diligently painting them. This is probably going to be an annual event."

"That would be nice," I said. "I need to run, Adam. See you Sunday." That just slipped out, like someone else said it. *What's up with that?* I thought.

✦ ✦ ✦

Early that afternoon, I called Evan Smith, friend and family doctor. His wife, Helena, and Mary were casual friends. She was not part of the Annie Oakleys. I guess she didn't have a gun carry permit. We had met them at the club for dinner a few times. Mary and I liked them, and we really didn't have any couple friends in Mountain Center. Evan's receptionist answered.

"Donald Youngblood for Dr. Smith," I said. "If he's busy, he can call me back."

"Hang on, Mr. Youngblood," she said.

Maybe a minute passed, and then Evan was on the line.

"You okay, Don?" he said. "Shot, stabbed, head bashed in?"

"Sorry to disappoint," I said. "I'm fine. I need you to do some medical snooping when you get a minute."

"Sure, as long as it doesn't violate confidentiality."

"It won't."

"Tell me what you need," Evan said.

"I need for you to find out if anything unusual occurred on the children's ward this week."

"Like what?"

"If I told you that, it would color your objectivity," I said. "Ask around and see what kind of response you get."

"Now you've really got me curious," he said. "I know one of the nurses well. I'll call you tomorrow."

✦ ✦ ✦

That night, I took Mary to the country club for dinner. We ordered drinks. I stared at her and smiled.

"What?" she said.

"You look gorgeous."

"Are you trying to get in my pants, Cowboy?"

"I've already been in your pants. But a return visit is always memorable."

Mary laughed. I loved her laugh.

"Hold that thought," she said. "Tell me about your day."

I told her about going by the church and talking to Adam. I told her about my phone call to Evan Smith. There wasn't much else. The rest of my day was boring.

"Evan must have been surprised," Mary said.

"And curious."

"I can almost see your wheels turning. What are you thinking?"

"Do you think there are people in the world with the power to heal?"

She was quiet for a moment. "Really?"

I nodded.

"Well, I suppose it's possible," she said. "Do you?"

"The Internet is full of healings and healers," I said. "Whether any of it's true or not is hard to prove."

"I guess some things you have to take on faith," Mary said. "But seeing is believing. I guess if I saw it, I'd believe it unless I suspected fraud."

"So, you're a doubting Thomas," I said.

"Aren't we all?"

"Most of us, I suspect. I've always thought healers were possible, that some humans have that power and just don't know how to tap into it."

"Are you thinking Jeremiah is a healer?" Mary said. "Is that why you called Evan?"

"I don't know what he is. I know he's a mystery I'd like to solve."

✦ ✦ ✦

Early the next morning, I parked and went directly down the alley to the back door of the diner. I slipped in and sat at my table. I half expected to see Jeremiah James sitting there. He wasn't.

Doris showed up with coffee and a preowned *Mountain Center Press* newspaper. "Alone?" she said.

"Looks that way," I said. "Bring me the usual."

"You got it," she said.

I opened the paper and found the sports section. In a few minutes, Doris returned with my food.

"Seen Jeremiah around?" I said.

"Oh, yes," Doris said. "He comes in often. I let him sit at your table. I hope that's okay."

"That's fine, Doris. But it's your table, not mine."

She patted me on the shoulder. "This has been your table for years, and that's never going to change. She walked away before I could protest. *Doris, you're as good as it gets*, I thought.

I ate slowly and read the paper. The police blotter seemed unusually light. I was close to finishing breakfast when Doris reappeared.

"Have you seen my front window?" she said as she refreshed my coffee.

"No, I haven't."

"Jeremiah painted a beautiful Christmas scene on it," Doris said. "Everyone comments on it when they come in. As payment, I told him he can eat free the rest of the year. He usually come in for dinner."

"That's very generous of you, Doris."

"It's nothing. We always have extra food at the end of the day."

"I'll go out the front door when I leave."

"You'll be amazed," she said, and hurried away to attend to other diners.

I finished my breakfast, left sufficient money on the table to cover the bill, walked through the diner, and exited by the front door. Outside, I turned around to look. What I saw was a detailed Christmas mural of a snowy countryside with a church and a few houses with some people sprinkled in—excellent work. At the top was a big "Merry Christmas" in flowing red letters. Amazing, for sure. Then again, nothing Jeremiah did really amazed me. Amazing was beginning to be the norm.

As I walked back to work, I noticed murals on other storefront windows—all different scenes, all Christmas themed, some with scripture references, all excellent. I wondered when Jeremiah found time to sleep.

14

December 15, ten days before Christmas

Friday, I was in early. *Ten days before Christmas,* I thought. *I'm going to have to do some shopping.* I spent the morning online looking at potential gifts on Amazon, then decided I would go to the mall next week and support the local shops. The office was quiet. I had coffee and watched the sparse traffic on Main Street.

Later, Gretchen and Rhonda came in and things were less quiet. Phones rang, printers printed, conversations took place. Cherokee Investigations was alive and well. I must admit I felt a sense of pride.

Midmorning, I got a surprise. Billy walked in.

"Well," I said, "what brings you to town?"

"Johnson City had a murder," he said. "Their chief called me in the middle of the night and asked me to come up and shoot the crime scene. Their regular guy is on vacation."

"Lucky you," I said.

Billy had done a lot of forensic photography in the area, but not so much anymore.

"Well, the pay is good," he said. "But I did it as a favor."

"So, who killed whom?"

"Who knows?" Billy said. "Looks like a drug deal gone bad. I shot the scene and kept my mouth shut."

"Are you going to start doing forensic photography again?"

"No," Billy said. "I'm a husband and father now. I don't need the extra money, and I don't need to have those images in my head."

"Don't blame you," I said.

Billy paused and looked out the window. He looked tired. "I hear there's a mystery guy in town you're somewhat obsessed with," Billy said.

"News travels fast among wives."

"It does," Billy said. "Want to tell me about it?"

I told Billy everything I'd learned about Jeremiah James since I first saw him at the Bloody Duck.

"So, he's good looking, he does great work, he volunteers his time, he seems to be spiritual, everyone likes him, and he might be a healer," Billy said. "That about sum it up?"

I said nothing.

"And you're skeptical and want to dig into his background," Billy said.

I shrugged.

"You're bored, Blood."

"True," I said. "But there's more to him than meets the eye. I'd like you to meet him."

"Maybe I'll bring Maggie and Little D over to see the live Nativity," Billy said.

"Do that. We'll go to the club afterward for dinner. You can stay overnight at the lake house or at the condo if you like."

"In that case, we may get a sitter. We don't get out much by ourselves, if you get my meaning."

"I do indeed," I said. "Go home and get some rest, Chief. And don't fall asleep driving over the mountain."

"Yes, Mother," Billy said.

That was my comment to him on many occasions in our past when he would worry about me. The roles were reversed. That was curious. I never worried about Billy. I smiled and shook my head.

✦ ✦ ✦

Billy was long gone when my cell phone rang near lunchtime. Caller ID informed me that it was Danny West.

"Danny," I said. "What have you got?"

"I found what you're looking for," he said. "Even made a few calls."

"Let's hear it."

"There was a Jeremiah James that died from a fall while rock climbing in 1964," Danny said. "I found an article on microfilm from the *Albuquerque Journal*. They're in the process of getting all their archives on computer files and are working their way backward.

They haven't gotten to 1964 yet. They were founded in 1880."

"They've got a lot more to do," I said. "What did the article say?"

"Not much. Just that he was twenty years old, was climbing alone, and died at the scene."

"Any follow-up articles?"

"Not that I could find."

"You said you made a few calls," I said. "Calls about what?"

"I was curious if they did an autopsy. So, I made some calls to track down who the coroner was at that time and found out that he's still alive. The guy must be eighty-five. Sounded fine on the phone until I mentioned Jeremiah James, then he was old and forgetful. Said he didn't remember him. I'd bet my paycheck he was lying."

"Good work, Danny," I said. "Send me a copy of the article and all the info you have on the coroner."

"Will do," Danny said.

"Where does he live?"

"He retired to Santa Fe. His name is Clarence Cutter. How's that for the name of a coroner?"

"I can hear it now," I said. "Clarence the cutter."

✦ ✦ ✦

I received the file from Danny West later in the day. Included were the address and phone number for retired coroner Clarence Cutter. Also included was the article from the *Albuquerque Journal*. I printed it. The piece was short and not so sweet.

Climber dies in Sandia Mountains

Jeremiah James, a 20-year-old rock climber, died yesterday from injuries sustained in a fall while rock climbing alone in Echo Canyon, a popular spot in the Sandia Mountains northeast of Albuquerque. James appeared to be climbing alone. He was found soon after his fall by nearby climbers. He was pronounced dead at the scene. The climb was described as a difficult one by the climbers who found his body. According to his driver's license, James was a native of Franklin, North Carolina.

I read it again. The article was dated June 28, 1964. Unfortunately, there was no photograph. I needed to talk with Clarence Cutter. I also needed a picture of our Jeremiah James without Jeremiah getting suspicious. I thought about that for a while. Then I called Gail Fields at the *Mountain Center Press*.

✦ ✦ ✦

Late that afternoon, Gail sat in my office in one of my oversized chairs, a curious look on her face. She had short, dark hair, dark brown eyes, and a pleasant girl-next-door face. Since I first met her, she had added some weight, and with it some curves in all the right places. I had to admit she looked good. I wondered if she had a gun carry permit.

"Okay, what is it?" she said. "You want something."

"I need you to do a story on the live Nativity at Mountain Center Methodist Church."

"They're having a live Nativity?"

"Yes."

"I guess I could do that," she said. "For you."

I ignored the little flirtation. "What I really want is a picture of a guy by the name of Jeremiah James. That part is strictly confidential. Jeremiah is in charge of building the Nativity. Get a picture of the work crew, and be sure Jeremiah is in it. Call Adam Church tonight and set it up."

"What's this about?"

"A Christmas surprise," I said. "Nothing sinister." *I hope*, I thought.

"What do I get?" Gail said.

"The next big scoop," I said. "When have I not been fair with you?"

"Okay, okay. That works. You've always kept me in the loop. I'll call Pastor Church as soon as I get back to the office."

15

We spent the weekend at the lake house. Mary was still asleep when I turned the dogs out in the side yard and made the quarter-mile walk to our mailbox for the Sunday paper. The day was cold and overcast. By the time I got back to the house, the dogs, especially Jake, were ready to come in.

I sat at the kitchen bar, drank coffee, and perused the paper. In the family section, I found an article on the live Nativity at Mountain Center Methodist Church and a nice picture of the work crew with Adam Church and Jeremiah James at the center. Everyone was smiling widely, like they were having a good time. The article had a lot of details that really didn't need to be there. I guessed that Jeremiah had worked his magic on Gail Fields.

"Nice article," Mary said, leaning over my shoulder. "And a good photo." Mary had seen the article from the *Albuquerque Journal*. It had piqued her curiosity.

"Good morning," I said.

"Coffee," Mary said.

"In your Yeti. Hot. Be careful."

"My hero," she said. She took a sip. "Perfect."

She knew what I was up to and was anxious to see what I could find out. I still felt a little guilty about investigating Jeremiah, but I was driven by the need to know exactly who the mystery man of Mountain Center was. "Be careful what you want," my mother used to say.

"Would you like some breakfast?" I said.

"Sure," Mary said. "What do you have in mind?"

"Bacon, challah bread French toast with nutmeg, and mimosas."

"What's for dessert?"

"I was hoping you'd ask," I said.

✦ ✦ ✦

Mary drove her truck to the late service at Mountain Center Methodist with me riding shotgun.

"You think we should ask forgiveness for having sex on a Sunday?" Mary said.

"We could ask Adam, but since we're married, I think it's okay."

"Let's leave Adam out of this," Mary said.

✦ ✦ ✦

During the announcements, Adam said, "Many of you have met Jeremiah James, who's building a full-sized stable and manger on our front lawn for our live

Nativity. We'll have live Nativity events on this coming Friday, Saturday, and Sunday at five o'clock, six o'clock, and seven o'clock. That's nine performances. Anyone who would like to volunteer to be part of any performance, please see Jeremiah. During those times the live Nativity is not being performed, life-sized Nativity figurines will take the place of the live Nativity. The Nativity work crew has been very busy with the assembly and painting of those figurines, and I can tell you that what I've seen so far is impressive. Jeremiah, please stand up."

Jeremiah stood from the front pew, looked back toward the congregation, and smiled. There was a polite round of applause. Jeremiah gave a little wave and sat down.

"Jeremiah has a sign-up sheet for participating, and I certainly hope you'll play a part in this wonderful undertaking," Adam continued. "Let's all help make this an inspiring event."

After the service, Jeremiah, carrying a clipboard, greeted Mary and me.

"I've got a spot for a Wise Man on Christmas Eve, Don," he said. "Can I put you down? You don't have to say anything. When it's time, you just come around the side of the building with the other Wise Men, present your gift to the Christ child, and wait near the stable until the final carol is sung."

"I think we have other plans," I said.

"It would mean a lot if you'd participate," he said. "A lot of people, young people especially, look up to you. It would be quite a testimony."

I looked at Mary for help.

"I believe we're free," Mary said. "Don would love to do it, wouldn't you?" Then she whispered in my ear, "There will be a big reward for you, Cowboy."

"I'll do it," I said to Jeremiah. *What a pushover!*

✦ ✦ ✦

After church, we drove to the outskirts of town to buy a Christmas tree from the local Civitan Club.

"You pick the tree," I said to Mary. Big mistake.

An hour later, after Mary had looked at every single tree on the lot, we bought a beautiful Douglas fir. We put it in the back of Mary's truck and drove to the lake house.

16

December 18, seven days before Christmas

Early Monday morning, Gail Fields dropped by my office. She came in, sat down, and handed me a Zip drive. She was full of energy.

"I knew you'd be in early," she said.

"Coffee?"

"Sure."

"Black?"

"Yes."

I popped in a Dunkin' Donuts K-Cup and a minute later handed Gail a freshly brewed hot coffee in a to-go cup. I didn't want her hanging around too long.

"Thanks," she said. She took a drink. "On that Zip drive are three photos. One is a fairly good close-up of Reverend Church and Jeremiah James. You didn't tell me he was so damn good looking."

"Down, Gail," I said. "He'll be gone before you know it."

"Maybe, but he's here now."

"Well, good luck. And thanks for the Zip drive."

"You're welcome," she said. "Got to run. Thanks for the coffee." She took her to-go cup and left.

✦ ✦ ✦

Later that morning, after looking at it, I gave the Zip drive to Gretchen.

"There are three photos on that drive," I said. "Jeremiah James is in all of them. Pick out the best candidate, scan it, manipulate it, and give me a full head shot of Jeremiah."

"You want to tell me what's going on?"

"No," I said. "It's personal."

"Is he dangerous?"

"Not that I can tell. Right now, he appears too good to be true."

"I think you're obsessing," Gretchen said. "What's Mary think?"

"Mary thinks I may be on to something."

"That's good enough for me," Gretchen said. "I'll get right on it."

✦ ✦ ✦

I had the head shot of Jeremiah James on my desk an hour later. Gretchen had done an excellent job. There was only one way I could proceed. I called Jim Doak, pilot *extraordinaire* of Fleet Industries jet number one. I was lucky enough to have access to the Fleet jet, and had for a long time. After all, I was on their board of directors.

"When can you fly me to Santa Fe?" I said when he answered.

"New Mexico?"

"There's more than one?"

"Twenty," Jim said. "Only two of them are in the United States. The other one is Santa Fe, Texas, population around fourteen thousand. Pilots seem to know that kind of useless information."

"I'm impressed. In my case, it's Santa Fe, New Mexico."

"I'm free tomorrow," he said. "Day trip?"

"I hope so."

"Eight o'clock at Tri-Cities," Jim said.

"I'll be there," I said.

17

December 19, six days before Christmas

At eight o'clock the next morning, I walked up the stairs of Fleet Industries jet number one carrying my laptop backpack and a brand-new Yeti twenty-ounce tumbler filled with hot coffee just the way I liked it. I had kept the old Yeti that stopped a sniper's bullet from killing me, but it was no longer suitable to hold hot coffee. The stairs closed behind me as I found my usual seat. Jim Doak was already in the cockpit.

"Buckle up, Don," he said over the intercom.

We taxied out to our takeoff position.

"Number one for takeoff," Jim said.

Moments later, we were speeding down the tarmac, and then I felt the earth drop away as we were airborne. The jet made a wide sweep to the west, and we were on our way to Santa Fe.

"Going to level off at thirty thousand feet," Jim said. "Should be smooth sailing. Relax and enjoy. We've got about three hours."

✦ ✦ ✦

By nine-fifteen Santa Fe time, we were on the ground and I was headed to pick up my rental, a white Lexus 460GX. Jim said he would wait with the jet and be ready to leave when I returned. I stopped at the Santa Fe Regional Airport grill before exiting the airport. I ordered a breakfast burrito minus the green chili, plus coffee. I checked out football news on my laptop while I leisurely ate my burrito.

Back in my rental, I programmed the GPS with the address Danny West had given me and pulled onto Aviation Drive. Fifteen minutes later, I parked in front of an upscale assisted living complex. I was expecting a single residence. Since Danny had not mentioned assisted living, I doubted he was aware. I walked inside like I knew what I was doing.

"I'm here to see Clarence Cutter," I said to the receptionist. She was middle-aged, attractive, and well dressed. "I'm an old family friend."

I was hoping Clarence had family. If not, I would have to go in a different direction. She never gave it a second thought.

"He's probably in the game room looking for someone to play checkers with," she said. "Do you play checkers?"

"Not in years," I said.

"Play a game or two with him," she said. "It will make his day."

"Sure. Which way to the game room?"

"Down that hall," she said, pointing. "You can't miss it."

The game room had a fireplace, three TVs, and a number of tables scattered about with comfortable-looking chairs. A round poker table was set up for five players; otherwise, the tables were square and set up for four. Some had checker/chess board inlays. A lean, lanky, white-haired man sat in the corner staring at the tabletop, which was set up for a game of checkers.

I walked over. "I heard you might be looking for a game," I said.

"You play?"

"I know how," I said. "I'm not that good."

"Have a seat," he said. "I'm Clarence."

"Don," I said.

We shook hands.

"Visitors go first," he said, nodding toward the board.

I moved a checker, and the game began. I wasn't much interested in winning or losing. I was more interested in finding a segue into the questions I wanted to ask. I shouldn't have worried.

"Been here long?"

"Few years," Clarence said. "I got tired of having to keep up a home. This is a nice place. The people are nice, the food is good, and I don't have to do anything I don't want to do."

Clarence won the first game easily.

"If you'll play harder this time, I'll tell you what you came to find out." He smiled, revealing a mouthful of perfect-looking teeth. His pale blue eyes twinkled, leaving me no doubt that Clarence Cutter was a sharp old bird.

"What makes you think I came to find out anything?"

"You've got detective written all over you," he said. "Are you on the local force?"

"No."

"Your move," he said.

We didn't talk. I concentrated on the game. I traded checkers as often as possible, and ten minutes later we were down to two kings each. I moved my kings away from each other so I wouldn't get trapped.

Clarence looked up and smiled. "Playing for a draw, I take it."

"I don't figure I can win, so I'm playing it safe."

"Draw?"

"Draw," I said.

"Thanks for humoring an old man," he said. "Tell me why you're here."

I slid the head shot of Jeremiah James across the table. "Look familiar?"

He studied it, then turned to me, his look a mixture of concern and curiosity. "Tell me who you are."

"A private detective from Tennessee," I said. "That's all you need to know."

He stared at the photo awhile longer. *Stalling*, I thought. *Trying to form a response.*

"When was this taken?"

"A few days ago," I said.

"Well, it can't be him," Clarence said. "But it sure as hell looks like him, or at least how I remember him."

"Who is *him*?"

"You know who," he said, pointing a bony finger at me. "Otherwise, you wouldn't be here."

"Tell me about him," I said.

"Tell me why you want to know."

"Between us?"

"Sure," he said. "Hell, who am I going to tell? Nobody cares about this anymore."

I didn't see any reason not to tell him about Jeremiah James and my trying to learn who he really was. As he said, who was he going to tell who cared? So, I left out Mountain Center and the name of anyone who was part of the story. I took my time. Clarence was most attentive.

"So, this ninety-year-old retired librarian in Jeremiah's hometown remembered that he was killed in a climbing accident out west, and that something happened to the body," I concluded. "A friend who's really good doing research led me to you."

"That's a hell of a story," Clarence said.

"Your turn," I said.

"You know, my memory isn't as good as it used to be," he said.

I said nothing. I gave him the best cop stare I could. Where was Mary when I needed her?

"But I'll never forget that face," he said, pointing at Jeremiah Johnson. "Must be a grandson."

"Maybe," I said. "Quit stalling."

"Just stretching it out a little. I don't get many visitors."

I waited.

"So, his grandfather or whoever he was arrives at the morgue late on a Friday in 1964—June, I think," Clarence Cutter began. "I'm about ready to go home. Climbing accident, they tell me. I unzip the body bag, and I'm shocked at how good looking this kid is and amazed there's not more damage that I can see. There has to be some, of course, but it's late and I don't take him out of the bag. I just store him in one of the coolers while the cops try to track down the next of kin. I come in on Monday and the body is gone. I ask around and no one knows where it went. I figure that maybe some funeral-home guys got it. So, I check and no one knows nothing. There were no security cameras in those days and no night watch-man. We can't ignore it because it's already on record and the paper ran an article about the accident."

"So, what happened?"

"The powers that be were worried about getting sued," Clarence said. "They still hadn't located the next of kin, so they got this idea to cremate a John Doe who'd been on ice for a month and pretend like the cremation was this James guy, and that it was a mistake. So, that's what they did. I guess they got away with it. I was sworn to secrecy and given a tidy little sum for my future retirement. That's how I can afford this place." All of a sudden, a strange look came over him. "You're not wired, are you?"

I laughed. "A little late to ask, isn't it?"

"Yeah, I guess it is," he chuckled.

"No wire," I said. "You're safe."

He relaxed and took a deep breath. "That's all I can tell you. No one ever found out what happened to that body."

"You're sure he was dead?"

He thought for a moment. "Not positive. Never got to fully examine him. But they had never sent me a live one."

"Were you at the scene?"

"No," he said. "In those days, we didn't go to the scene unless it was suspicious."

"Fingerprints?"

"No. I was going to do that first thing Monday when I examined the body. I just could not believe someone took it."

"Maybe someone sold it to a med school," I said.

"One of my first thoughts," Clarence said. "One of our police detectives, in the loop, checked out every possibility within two hundred miles."

"Okay, what if he wasn't dead? Could he have gotten out of the body bag and the locker without help?"

"No way," Clarence said. "I thought of that, too. I tried and couldn't do it. He would have needed help."

"You've thought about this a lot," I said.

"It bugged the hell out of me for years."

I played a couple of more games of checkers with Clarence, then left, feeling I was no closer to finding out who Jeremiah James really was. No fingerprints, no DNA, and no leads.

✦ ✦ ✦

By the time I got to the jet and we flew back to Mountain Center, it was dark. I called Mary while I was driving to the condo.

"I'm back," I said. "On my way from the airport. See you in about half an hour."

"I'll have dinner waiting," Mary said.

✦ ✦ ✦

We had a leisurely dinner at the kitchen bar. Mary had prepared a chicken casserole with broccoli and water chestnuts, accompanied by mashed potatoes and a tossed salad. I gave her the ultimate compliment: I had seconds.

"What kind of guy was Clarence Cutter?" Mary asked.

"Old, interesting, and sharp," I said. "He saw right through me." I told her about my visit.

Mary laughed. "You played checkers?"

"I did. Checkers was the coin of the realm. The games bought me the information I needed."

"This whole thing is just a little bit weird," Mary said. "I think it's time to stop and enjoy the holidays. Accept the facts: Jeremiah is a really nice guy, although a bit mysterious."

"I think you're right," I said. "I'm done."

18

December 21, four days before Christmas

Two days later, I was in the office early. I had awakened in a panic, realizing it was the Thursday before Christmas and I had not done any Christmas shopping. I had slept in on Wednesday and spent most of the day organizing the boathouse.

My plan was to go to the mall after lunch. I knew it would be crowded, but I would have to deal with it. I had spent too much time trying to unravel Jeremiah James, man of mystery. I brewed coffee and ate a large blueberry muffin Mary had made. I was about to boot up my desktop computer when the phone rang.

"Youngblood," I answered without thinking. Not very professional, but technically we weren't open yet.

"Don, it's Evan Smith."

"Hey, Doc." I had forgotten my phone call to Evan asking him to do a little snooping around the children's ward. "What's up?"

"I have no idea what's up," he said. "All I know is that you are somehow in tune to what amounts to minor and major medical miracles in the children's ward."

I sat straight up in my chair. "Tell me."

"There were twelve kids of various ages in the children's ward on Monday of last week in various stages of treatment, mostly for cancer," Evan Smith said. "All of them are now home for Christmas. Every one showed remarkable improvement during the week. The most astonishing was a kid with acute leukemia who on Thursday showed no signs of the disease. I spoke directly with his doctor. He said it was a miracle. Don, he was in tears when he told me. He said the kid maybe had a year to live. He could not believe it. He ran the test three times to confirm. Other kids are either showing great improvement, healing faster than expected from injuries, or are in remission from cancer. Please tell me what's going on."

"I can't," I said. "I don't know what's going on, only what I suspect. I don't want to talk about it over the phone. Come by the office when you get off and we'll talk."

"I'll do that," Evan Smith said. "Whatever this is, Don, I'm not complaining."

✦ ✦ ✦

Later that morning, Lacy called.

"What did you get Mom for Christmas?"

"Well . . ."

"You haven't gotten her a thing, have you?"

"I'm going shopping this afternoon."

"Okay," she said. "Let me tell you what not to get her."

"All right," I said when she finished. "That helps. Duly noted."

"Have you put up the tree?"

"Not yet."

"Is there a tree?" *The third degree!*

"Yes," I said, "there is a tree. Mary looked at every tree on the Civitan lot and picked out the best one, according to her."

"Good," she said. "We'll all decorate it together."

"When are you coming?"

"Tomorrow night," Lacy said. "We're renting a car and staying with Biker's parents. We'll come to the lake house Saturday morning and decorate the tree. Do you have it at the lake house?"

"Yes."

"Okay, that's good," Lacy said. "See you then. Love you."

"Love you, too," I said.

Why do I feel like I'm dealing with Mary? I thought.

✦ ✦ ✦

After lunch, I went to the mall. Parking spots anywhere close to the main entrance were nonexistent, so I parked as far away as I could to avoid having to squeeze between cars. As I walked toward the large double doors, I heard the familiar ring of the Salvation

Army bell. A man I recognized from Mountain Center Methodist Church stood smiling at passersby, trying to engage eye contact. He was having only moderate success. Many looked away. He had on a red apron and a Santa Claus hat. I took a twenty from my wallet and dropped it in his red kettle.

"Thank you very much, Mr. Youngblood," he said. "Have a Merry Christmas."

"You, too," I said. *I've been in the paper way too much*, I thought.

The mall manager had made small shopping carts available with the idea that it might improve sales if customers didn't have to carry their purchases from store to store. This clever idea certainly worked for me. I had purchases in my cart from Victoria's Secret, Godiva Chocolatier, Kay Jewelers, and The Wine Shop. Standing in front of The Music Store, I saw Jeremiah James in the distance talking to a young couple from church. I was wheeling toward them to say hello when I heard gunfire and screams.

I left my cart and ran toward Jeremiah, but he was already on the move toward the gunfire. I could tell it was not an automatic weapon. The shots sounded more like those of a nine millimeter. I had just about caught up with Jeremiah when I saw the shooter. He was a skinny young man with dark, spiked hair, wild eyes, and a bewildered look. From under the back of my jacket, I pulled my Beretta nine millimeter. I was almost past Jeremiah when he threw out an arm and stopped me. He took my gun hand by the wrist and pushed it down. For some unexplained reason, I didn't resist. The shooter was about ten yards from Jeremiah, walking slowly, when he took aim and pulled the trigger. I tried to break free from Jeremiah's grip, but it was as if my arm were paralyzed. All I could do was watch. The shooter's hand was shaking, and the shot missed. Jeremiah stretched out his arm toward the shooter like he was stiff-arming a tackler and said in a calm but stern voice, "*Sad, beshm jezus hanutseri, yealem.*"

The shooter stopped in his tracks with a look like he had seen the most terrifying thing in his life. His eyes were wild and his face contorted.

"Put the gun down," I said loudly.

He didn't. He put the gun to his head and pulled the trigger. Then a shadow seemed to rise from the floor and pass overhead like a cloud blocking the sun before it disappeared into the roof of the mall. I wasn't even sure I had seen what I thought I saw. Jeremiah ran past the shooter, ignoring him, and down the mall toward the victims lying on the floor. I stood watching as he knelt and touched each one briefly, said something, and moved on. I put the Beretta away and called Big Bob's cell as I heard sirens in the distance.

"I'm busy, Blood," he said hurriedly.

"I'm at the mall," I said. "The shooter is dead and no longer a threat. Tell your guys not to shoot anyone. Send ambulances."

"Stay put," he said.

I called Evan Smith's cell. "Get to the emergency room now," I said.

"Don?"

"Just do it," I said. "Stay until I get there."

"Leaving now," he said.

Minutes later, Jeremiah was back standing beside me.

"What just happened?" I said.

"What do you think just happened?"

"I think you saved a lot of people."

"If I hadn't been here, you would have saved them, Don."

"How did you know he'd miss? You could have been killed," I said.

He ignored me. "I think I'd better go. I would rather not answer any questions at this point. Before I leave Mountain Center, I'll tell you everything you want to know, and maybe some things you don't."

For some unexplained reason, all I said was, "Go."

"See you Christmas Eve," Jeremiah said as he walked away.

People began coming out of their hiding places. Mountain Center policemen and paramedics arrived. An announcement came over the loudspeaker: "Attention. The mall is closed for the remainder of the day. Please exit at once. Repeat. The mall is closed for the remainder of the day. Please exit at once."

I knew that closing the mall four days before Christmas was not going to sit well with the shop owners. Shoppers began filing to the exits. Shopkeepers began closing. I stood watching, trying to process what I had just seen. How could I be involved in another mass shooting in less than a year? What was that shadow I thought I had seen? What kind of mystical power did Jeremiah James possess? The dead shooter lay in his own blood not thirty feet from where I was standing. He was definitely not a terrorist. No body armor and no automatic weapon. A disillusioned crazy person.

My cell phone rang.

"I just got paged to go to the mall ASAP," Mary said. "What's happening?"

"Shooter," I said. "It's under control. I'll call you later." I disconnected before she could ask more questions.

I heard the big man coming from behind me as he walked across a patch of marble floor, the leather heels of the boots he always wore signaling his arrival. He stopped beside me.

"Did you do that?" he said, looking at the shooter.

"Self-inflicted," I said.

"Did he say anything?"

"Not a word. I think he was on something. He looked like a wild man. I had my Beretta out ready to fire when he offed himself."

I was telling the truth, although not the whole truth. I was hoping that everyone had been running for their lives and hadn't seen Jeremiah.

In the distance, I saw Sean, Big Bob's brother, walking hurriedly toward us.

"The mall is secure," he said. "Seven people shot, a few seriously, maybe one dead."

"The mall at Christmastime," Big Bob said to no one in particular. "What's the world coming to when Christmas shopping becomes dangerous?"

I didn't have an answer. I retrieved my shopping cart and went to my SUV wondering what the odds were that anyone would see two random shooters commit suicide in the same year.

19

December 21, still four days before Christmas

At the hospital emergency room, I asked for Evan Smith.

"He's really busy right now, Mr. Youngblood," the receptionist said. I didn't know her, but she obviously knew me.

"When you have an opportunity, tell him I'm here," I said. "I'll be in the waiting room."

"I certainly will," she said. "Were you at the mall?"

"I was," I said. News in a small town traveled faster than a Kentucky thoroughbred.

"Terrible," she said.

"Yes, it was." I turned and walked away before she could say anything else. I didn't want to answer questions.

As I headed toward the waiting room, my cell phone rang.

"Where are you?" Mary said.

"At the hospital checking on victims. I'm waiting to have a conversation with Evan. Are you at the mall?"

"Yes, but I'll be heading home soon. Anyone dead?"

"Not sure," I said. "I'll tell you all about it when I get home."

"Okay," Mary said. "Don't stay any longer than you have to. I need you with me."

✦ ✦ ✦

A half-hour later, Evan Smith came out. "Come with me," he said.

He led me to a consulting room. We sat down. He looked tired.

An attractive young nurse came right behind us carrying two cups of coffee with lids. She handed one to Evan. "Dr. Smith," she said, "you look like you could use this."

"Thank you, Jane," he said. "That's very thoughtful."

She handed the second cup to me. "Mr. Youngblood. Half-and-half with two sugars."

"Thanks so much," I said. "You're a mind reader and a lifesaver."

She smiled and closed the door on her way out.

Evan took a drink of his coffee.

"Cream and two sugars?" I said. "How'd she know?"

"You're a celebrity around here," he said.

"Well, I've certainly been here enough."

"True." He drank more coffee and then said, "Thanks for calling me. Two of the wounded are regular patients of mine, so I took over their cases. One should be dead but isn't."

"Did anyone die?"

"No," Evan said. "One of my patients should have, and I cannot explain why she didn't. There's a bullet behind her heart. It's like it passed through her heart without doing any damage. Also, her blood loss was not nearly as much as it should have been. Last but not least, she's conscious and swears she was dead and that someone brought her back."

At this point, I'll believe anything, I thought. I said nothing.

"I have a feeling you're not surprised," Evan Smith said, as if reading my mind.

"I've come to the conclusion that it's best not to question miracles. If I can ever share any solid facts, I will. Until then, I'm chalking it up to divine intervention."

"That's about all it could be," Evan Smith said, finishing his coffee. "Now, I'm going home, sharing a glass of wine with my lovely wife, and getting some rest."

"There's a thought I can wrap my mind around," I said.

✦ ✦ ✦

By the time I left the hospital, night was falling, aided by a thick cloud cover. I drove to the office and took my packages up the back stairs to the second floor. No lights were on behind the door that read, **Cherokee Investigations**. To the right, a small plaque said, **Donald Youngblood, Senior Investigator**. Under my name was **Gretchen Graves, Investigator**. Under Gretchen's name was **Rhonda Sharkey, Investigator**. I stood looking at the plaque for a few seconds. *I've come a long way since the Fleet case*, I thought. I managed to get the door open without dropping anything and set Mary's gifts on the conference table.

I turned on a few lights and went into my office, where I turned on a few more lights. I went back to the outer office and moved all the packages into a closet in my private office. I looked for messages on my desk. None. Then I called Mary.

"I'll be home soon," I said.

"Put the pedal to the metal, Cowboy," she said. "The wine and I are waiting."

✦ ✦ ✦

Even though I was late for our normal cocktail hour, Mary didn't start without me. A bottle of a good, full-bodied red blend was alive and breathing on the kitchen bar. Cheese and crackers sat near the bottle. I sat down, and Mary poured stemless goblets half full of the red elixir. We clinked the goblets and drank.

"How did you manage to be at the mall for a shooting?" Mary said. "I can't let you out of my sight for one second."

"Just lucky," I said, although I had my doubts.

Mary gave me the cop stare.

"I was shopping," I said. "For you."

"That's okay, then. Tell me what happened."

I told her in as much detail as I could remember, including Jeremiah's part and what I thought I saw afterward.

"I didn't tell Big Bob," I said.

"Good call," Mary said. "He's not much into the mystical." She was quiet for a while. "Who is he, Don?"

"I don't know. But whoever or whatever he is, he seems to have special gifts, and he seems to be using them in a good way." I told her what Evan Smith had said to me about the miracle on the children's ward.

"Please tell me you're going to leave this alone."

"I am for now," I said. "I just want to enjoy Christmas without any more drama. Jeremiah promised to answer all my questions before he leaves."

"Well, that's good," Mary said.

I ate a cube of cheddar cheese, followed it with a cracker, and chased it with wine.

"The live Nativity starts tomorrow night," Mary said. "When is your Wise Man part?"

"Christmas Eve, I think. I want to go tomorrow night and have a look."

"Me, too," Mary said. "And then we'll go to the club for dinner."

"It's a date, Doll."

Mary laughed, a sound I needed to hear more of, given the day I'd had.

20

December 22, three days before Christmas

Friday morning, I parked behind my office building and walked up the alley to the back employee entrance of the Mountain Center Diner. I slipped in and took a chair at my reserved table so I could see the front entrance and most of the people inside. It didn't take long for Doris to spot me and bring a mug of hot coffee and a preowned *Mountain Center Press*. I stirred cream and sugar into the mug and opened the paper. I took a drink and began reading. "Shooting at Mountain Center Mall," the headline read. The article began,

```
A gunman, yet to be identified, opened fire
yesterday afternoon in the Mountain Center
Mall just after 2 p.m. Seven people were
wounded, two seriously. According to police,
the shooter, who witnesses described as in
his mid-to-late twenties, was carrying a Glock
nine-millimeter pistol. He emptied the entire
clip, saving the last bullet for himself, a
fatal shot to the head. At this time, it is
believed that the shooter acted alone.
```

The story went on to list the victims, the locations in the mall where they were shot, and a quote from Big Bob: "No comment at this time. It's an ongoing investigation."

No sooner did I turn to the sports page than the big man slipped in the back door and sat down across from me.

"You look tired," I said.

"I should look tired," he said. "I've been up most of the night ramrodding the investigation. I've had a meeting with the mayor and the town council about how to beef up security at the mall. The likelihood of another shooting is minimal, but we need to have a show of force to make people feel safe. I've talked to Jimmy Durham and the Johnson City and Greeneville chiefs to see if any of their men are interested in moonlighting. I've had a meeting with my own guys to encourage them to work overtime. And I've been to the hospital to question witnesses, some of whom I didn't get to talk with. This is going to blow my budget all to hell, but the mayor and town council have approved it."

"Let me buy you breakfast."

"Gladly," he said.

Doris showed up with more coffee. She was unusually quiet. She took our orders and left without comment.

"Have you identified the shooter?"

"We have," he said. He took a long drink of coffee. "Ex-military with PTSD. We'll know more after Wanda finishes with him, but from all accounts he was high on drugs."

"That would be my guess," I said. "Any criminal record?"

"None," Big Bob said. "And a good military record with a sharpshooter medal. We're lucky no one died."

Luck had nothing to do with it, I thought.

Big Bob drank more coffee and took a deep breath. He stared off into space like a man trying to remember something. I thought he might nod off. I waited and said nothing.

"The thing is, nobody seems to remember anything," he said. "Everyone was running or seeking cover. The security camera that would have shown the shooter offing himself was out. The guy who monitors the cameras said it was working when he came in."

"Weird," I said.

Doris materialized out of thin air, put our breakfast down, said "Enjoy," and hurried off. I often wondered why my food, and that of anyone else at my table, seemed to arrive so fast. My theory was that those orders went to the head of the line.

"What I want to know is why you didn't shoot the guy," Big Bob said. "You usually shoot first and deal with the fallout later. You certainly had the opportunity."

"He never pointed his gun at me," I said. "And he was far enough away that I couldn't risk missing him and hitting someone else farther down the mall. I told him to put the gun down. He looked like he was about to surrender, and then he quickly put the gun to his head and pulled the trigger."

I was bending the truth a little. Better that than trying to explain the miracle in the Mountain Center Mall.

Big Bob continued to eat. "There's something you're not telling me," he said. "I can always tell."

"I've told you all I can. Calm down and eat."

He gave me a hard stare and went back to his food. He finished his breakfast without another word.

"Go get some rest," I said. "If you need Mary and me to take a shift at the mall, we will."

He smiled. "She already volunteered."

"For both of us?"

"Of course," he said.

✦ ✦ ✦

Back in the office, I got a phone call I didn't expect.

"Joseph Fleet on line one," Gretchen said over the intercom.

"How's your day going?" he said when I picked up.

"Too soon to tell."

"I heard you were at the mall when the shooting occurred," he said.

It never ceased to amaze me how news traveled so fast in a small town.

"I was about thirty feet from the shooter with my gun out when he shot himself in the head," I said. "I'll spare you the details."

"I'm sorry you had to see that," Joseph Fleet said. "You've seen enough already in your lifetime."

"True enough. Are you still in Mountain Center?"

"I am. Oscar is going to drive me down after New Year's. I'd like to put together a little dinner party on Christmas Day. You and Mary, Billy and Maggie, Stanley Johns, Lacy and Biker, if they want to come, T. Elbert, Roy, of course, and anyone else you can think of. Sorry about the short notice."

"I'll talk to everyone and let you know," I said. "I think it will work. What made you decide to leave later?"

"I don't know," he said. "For some reason, I wasn't ready to go."

"There's one other person I'd like to invite. You'll like him. He'll fit right in."

"That's fine," he said. "Let me know how many to prepare for. No need to call Stanley. He's already said yes. Let's say around four o'clock."

"I'll be in touch," I said.

✦ ✦ ✦

Later that morning, I called Mary. "Got a second?" I said.

"Actually, I do," Mary said. "I'm getting caught up on some paperwork. The bad guys of Mountain Center seem to be taking the holidays off. Crime is down in our little town. What's going on?"

I told her about Joseph Fleet's invitation.

"Sounds good," she said. "I'll call Maggie. You call T. Elbert. Lacy and Biker will be at Biker's parents', so they probably won't come."

I hung up and called T. Elbert. "How would you like to join us for Christmas dinner at the Fleet mansion?" I said.

"You already know the answer to that," he said. "What time?"

"We're to be there around four o'clock," I said. "I'll pick you up around three forty-five."

"Easier if I drive the Black Beauty," T. Elbert said. "I'll see you there."

21

December 22, still three days before Christmas

That night, Mary and I went to Mountain Center Methodist Church to see the live Nativity. The night was cold and clear, but that didn't stop hundreds of people from showing up, including Billy, Maggie, and Little D. The Nativity was lit up but empty except for a tied-up cow and goat. They seemed content to be there. The first show was at five o'clock, as darkness turned the day to twilight.

At exactly five o'clock, the lights went out. Moments later, a spotlight shone on a young woman far to the left of the stable, who looked to be pregnant.

Jeremiah's voice came from hidden speakers: "Before Mary and Joseph married, Mary was found to be with child from the Holy Spirit."

He sounded as rich and clear as any professional I had ever heard. The spotlight on Mary dimmed and another, farther left, shone on a young man.

Again, Jeremiah's voice: "Joseph was not happy but did not wish to embarrass Mary, seeking a private way to dissolve the union. But an angel of the Lord came to Joseph in a dream and told Joseph to take Mary as his wife, for she carried the child of the Holy Spirit, which was a son to be named Jesus."

The young man playing Joseph bowed his head and closed his eyes. His spotlight dimmed. Out of the shadows came a young woman dressed as an angel, who whispered in Joseph's ear. She faded back into the shadows as Joseph awakened. Both spotlights brightened, and Mary and Joseph walked toward each other and embraced. Their spotlights faded again, and they disappeared into a nearby tent set up for the production.

Off to the right of the stable, a spotlight suddenly appeared on a group of carolers singing "It Came Upon a Midnight Clear," proclaiming the birth of Christ the savior. They finished, and their spotlight dimmed. Another spotlight came on, and from the back of the tent emerged Mary sitting on a donkey led by Joseph.

Jeremiah narrated, "And it came to pass that in those days a decree went out from Caesar Augustus that all the world should be taxed, everyone in his own city. So, Joseph took Mary, heavy with child, to Bethlehem."

Joseph slowly led the donkey into the stable. The spotlight dimmed, and a curtain was drawn around the stable. The spotlight on the carolers brightened as they sang "O Little Town of Bethlehem." As they finished, their spotlight dimmed again. The curtain around the stable was pulled away, and the spotlight brightened to reveal Mary, no longer pregnant, rocking a lifelike baby doll wrapped in a blanket, beside a manger filled with straw.

Jeremiah continued, "And In Bethlehem, Mary delivered her firstborn son. And she wrapped him in swaddling clothes and laid him in a manger, for there was no room at the inn."

The spotlight brightened on the carolers, who sang "Away in a Manger." They finished the carol, and their spotlight faded again. A spotlight once again shone on the place behind the tent, where now emerged the three Wise Men. At the same time they made their appearance, a star was illuminated, shining bright from high up on the side of the church.

Jeremiah concluded, "And there came from the east three Wise Men following a star that led them to the manger in Bethlehem. And they bore gifts of gold, frankincense, and myrrh."

The carolers, spotlighted again, sang "We Three Kings" as the Wise Men slowly made their way to the manger. They knelt before the baby and placed their gifts by the manger. When the carol was finished, they rose and moved away into the darkness and around the other side of the church, out of sight. The carolers then sang "Hark! The Herald Angels Sing."

When the carol was over, Pastor Adam stepped from the shadows and said, "That concludes our first program. Peace be with you. Thank you all for coming."

There was a loud round of applause. The crowd leisurely dispersed, though many stayed to chat with friends and others gathered around Jeremiah to offer congratulations.

"We're going back," Billy said. "I wanted Little D to see this. We'll stay over after the Christmas dinner at the Fleet mansion."

I rubbed Little D's head and said, "How are you doing, pal?"

"Good," he said. Like his father, he was a man of few words.

We said our goodbyes, and Billy, Maggie, and Little D walked away to their SUV.

A few minutes later, Jeremiah spotted us and broke away from the crowd. "Nice to see you two," he said.

"Thank you," Mary said. "The live presentation was inspiring."

"Very well done," I said.

"Thank you," Jeremiah said. "Was that your Cherokee friend from college that you told me about?"

"Yes," I said. "And his wife and little boy."

"Named after Don," Mary added.

"Nice," Jeremiah said. "Think you can handle one of the Wise Men parts, Don?"

With Mary's help, I had already said yes. Maybe Jeremiah was looking for confirmation. "Sure, why not?" I said. "Looks simple enough. When?"

"Seven o'clock on Christmas Eve, the last show," Jeremiah said. "Arrive about six-thirty so we can get you dressed."

"We'll be here," Mary said.

"Great," Jeremiah said. "See you then, if not before." He walked away to chat with other attendees.

"You continue to surprise me," Mary said.

"I continue to surprise myself. But if I remember correctly, you did volunteer me."

"Still," she said, "I never thought you'd do it."

22

December 23, two days before Christmas

Saturday morning at the lake house was cold. I was up early and dressed. Sleeping in was not in my DNA. Mary evidently had the sleep-in gene; she was still asleep, and so were the dogs. I didn't expect them to be up for at least an hour. I drank my first mug of coffee in my tiny office and then made the long, brisk walk up, over, and down the driveway to get the morning paper. I was in the den in a comfortable chair with coffee and the paper when my cell phone rang. **Private caller** showed on my screen.

"Who's calling so early in the morning?" I said.

"Relax, it's only the FBI."

"Am I in trouble?"

"All the time, it seems," David Steele said. "I figured you'd be up. What do you know about the shooting down there?"

"Just about everything," I said.

"You're not going to tell me you were an eyewitness."

"Both eyes," I said. "Up close and personal."

"I don't know how you do it. You're like a magnet for trouble. Tell me how it went down."

"Not much to tell," I said. "I was Christmas shopping. I heard the shots, went to investigate. I saw him coming toward me. I drew my Beretta, which, given my history, I carry all the time. About the time he got close enough that I could safely take a shot, he saved me the trouble by shooting himself in the head."

If I withheld information from the Mountain Center chief of police, I might as well withhold information from the deputy director of the FBI. After all, the shooter was dead. Why complicate things?

"Not a terrorist?"

"No," I said. "Supposedly a vet with PTSD, probably strung out on something. I'm staying out of it unless you want me to look into it."

"I'd be interested in what the tox report says," David Steele said. "Other than that, I see no reason for the FBI to get involved. Sounds like an isolated incident. If you think different, let me know."

"Will do," I said.

✦ ✦ ✦

Wanda Jones was a good friend, a huge flirt, and the second-best-looking woman in Mountain Center. She was also the county medical examiner. She and Mary were close friends, so the flirting had calmed down somewhat. I called her cell phone.

"Don. Everything okay?"

"You mean other than the shooting at the mall?" I said. "Yeah, everything is fine. Are you at the office?"

"Yes," she said. "I had to finish this today. I won't be back in the office until after New Year's."

"Do you have a tox report yet on the shooter?"

"I do," Wanda said. "I just finished it. But I can't give it to just any Tom, Dick, or Harry off the street. Is this official business?"

She was messing with me for sure. I played along.

"No," I said. "Not yet. But I have been asked to find out on behalf of the deputy director of the FBI."

"So, you're not on the case, but you might be," Wanda said.

"Something like that. What can you tell me?"

"Well, since it's you and Mary's my best friend, I guess I can tell you."

"Quit stalling, Wanda," I said, feigning annoyance.

"Okay," she said. "He was on crack cocaine and amphetamines. At the time of the shooting, he was probably angry, agitated, and maybe hallucinating. My guess would be he planned to kill himself all along."

"Thanks, Wanda."

"My pleasure, handsome," she said.

"Watch the flirting," I said. "You're betrothed."

"You're so easy to flirt with," she said. "And I have Mary's permission."

"Lucky me," I said. "Do you have plans for Christmas?"

"I do," Wanda said.

"In Vegas?"

"Yes, sir."

"Tell Bruiser hello," I said.

Dennis "Bruiser" Bracken, friend since college and Wanda's fiancé, was back and forth between Las Vegas and Mountain Center. Bruiser earned his nickname when he played football for the University of Connecticut and later for the Washington Redskins before they became the Washington Football Team. Their wedding date was a moving target, hard to pin down.

"I will," she said. "And you and that hot babe of yours have a good holiday."

"You're bad," I said. "Safe travels."

✦ ✦ ✦

Mary finally rolled out of bed around nine o'clock. She looked fetching as ever. I sat on a barstool and watched as she prepared a mug of coffee and toasted a blueberry muffin.

"What time did you get up?" Mary said.

"Hours ago. Remember, Lacy and Biker are coming soon to decorate the tree."

"Oh, shit," Mary said. "I'd better go make myself presentable."

"You look fine," I said.

"You're just a horny old man."

"I'll show you who's old," I said, sliding off the barstool.

I reached for her, and she pushed me away.

"Show me later, Cowboy. Get the decorations and the stand out of storage. When Lacy and Biker get here, you and Biker get the tree in the house and put it in the same place we used last year."

"Yes, ma'am," I said, saluting.

Mary turned, hurried down the hall toward the front door, took a hard right, and pounded up the stairs to the master bedroom.

✦ ✦ ✦

Lacy and Biker showed up an hour later. Biker and I went outside to get the tree ready for the stand. To make it fit, I had to remove a few lower branches. Then I sawed off about an inch from the stub and drilled a hole up the middle of the trunk with my portable drill. With a screwdriver, I wedged in a piece of an old T-shirt, which would act as a wick. We then attached the stand to the tree and stood it up on the front walk to make sure it was straight. After a few minor adjustments, we were satisfied.

I went inside to see if the females were ready for us to place the tree. Christmas music was playing on the CD player. Mary and Lacy had cleared the spot for the tree and laid down plastic. After the tree was in place, we would cover the stand with a white fuzzy blanket. If you used your imagination, you might convince yourself it was snow.

Biker and I carefully brought the tree in and placed it in the center of the plastic. We were given instructions to rotate it this way and that. Finally, after viewing the tree from all angles, Mary and Lacy were satisfied.

"Nice tree, Mom," Lacy said. "Don would have just grabbed the first one he saw."

"He would," Mary said.

"Now, hold on a minute," I said.

Everyone laughed except me.

Biker and I wrapped the blanket, then strung the lights and turned them on. Thankfully, they all worked. They should have, since they were almost new. All our old lights and ornaments were lost in the fire that took the old lake house. We'd had only a few Christmases since the fire to accumulate decorations.

Once the lights were on and approved by Mary and Lacy, they started hanging ornaments. Biker and I stood by and watched; our help no longer needed. The mood was festive, mixed with an air of sadness when we remembered lost ornaments from long ago, many from my childhood. After the final ornaments were in place, I added water to the stand, and we stood back and admired our work.

"Beautiful," Mary said.

"Perfect," Lacy said.

"Not bad," Biker said.

"All of the above," I said.

✦ ✦ ✦

We were hanging around the kitchen bar having brunch when the house phone rang.

"Who could that be?" Mary said, to herself more than anyone else. She lifted the phone out of its cradle, looked at caller ID, and said, "Mountain Center Methodist Church." The she pressed the on button and said, "Hello." Pause. "Hello, Adam." Pause.

"I'm fine. How are you?" Pause. "I can imagine." Pause. "What would we have to do?" Pause. "I see. Which service?" Pause. "The eleven o'clock would probably work better for us. Hang on a second, please. Let me confirm this with Don and Lacy." Mary put her hand over the mouthpiece of the portable phone. "He wants us as a family to do the Advent candle lighting Sunday morning. There's a short liturgy which we'll share."

"Sounds great," Lacy said. "Let's do it."

Mary looked at me.

"Fine," I said. I really had no other option.

Mary removed her hand and said, "Adam, we would love to do it. Thank you for asking." Pause. "Okay, see you then." She turned the phone off and placed it back on the cradle. "Well, that was nice."

"You-all have been going to church?" Lacy said.

"Ever since Thanksgiving," Mary said.

Lacy looked at me.

"Long story," I said.

"Let's hear it," Lacy said.

"Another time," I said. "Now that the tree is done, I have to go to the office for a little while."

"For what?" Mary said.

"Don't be so nosy," I said.

"Presents," Lacy said.

I smiled and said nothing.

23

December 23, still two days before Christmas

Mary was going to take Lacy and Biker to the mall so they could do some last-minute shopping. At the same time, she was taking a security shift. She was getting ready as I was leaving. She donned a dark blue bulletproof vest embroidered with *MCPD*. Her blond hair was in a ponytail pulled through the back of a baseball cap. The cap displayed the same logo as the vest. On her hip was a Glock Ten.

"I think the mall will be safe this afternoon," I said.

"Total badass," Lacy said, not hiding the admiration in her voice.

"Total," Biker said.

"Stay safe," I said.

I left the lake house and drove into Mountain Center. In the office, I turned on a few lights and checked the notes on my desk. One I had made for myself was a reminder to call Joseph Fleet back about the Christmas dinner guest list. Mary had confirmed that Billy and Maggie said yes. I rang Joseph Fleet's cell and got his voice mail: "If you called the right number, you know who this is. Leave a message."

"I've got six for dinner on my end, plus you, Stanley, and Roy make nine," I said. "Call me if you have any questions. If not, I'll see you around four on Christmas Day."

In no hurry to leave, enjoying the peace and quiet, I went online and surfed the web. Much later, I gathered Mary's presents, closed up, and went down the back stairs to my SUV. On my way out of town, I decided to go by the church. I wanted to see the Nativity with the life-sized figurines.

✦ ✦ ✦

From the street, the Nativity looked impressive. I parked the SUV, got out, and walked over to take a closer look. The carving and painting of the life-sized figures were exceptional. Mary, Joseph, baby Jesus, a donkey, a lamb, and a shepherd boy adorned the stable. I felt a presence behind me.

"What do you think?" he said.

"Amazing. How did you find time to do all of this?"

"I had help," Jeremiah said. "It didn't take as long as you might think. I did most of the carving with a small chainsaw. I added the details with some small tools and a rotary sander and then a hand sander. I had a work crew from the church that watched and picked up on what I was doing. Each figure took less and less time. Then we painted and lacquered them. I'm very pleased with how they turned out."

"You should be," I said. "Where did you get the wood?"

"One of the parishioners had cut down some pine trees this fall and hadn't finished cleaning them up," Jeremiah said. "He shredded the small stuff but still had some of the bigger logs lying around. Pine is excellent for chainsaw carving."

"That was fortunate."

"The Lord provides," Jeremiah said.

I didn't know how to respond to that, so I said nothing. We were quiet for a while as I took a closer look at each figurine. The workmanship was incredible.

"I've got to move these soon and get ready for tonight's live Nativity," Jeremiah said.

"I could help with that," I said.

"No need. I've got volunteers coming in later. Another way to get people involved. Are you ready for tomorrow? I hear the Youngbloods are lighting the Advent candles in the late-morning service."

"Mary and Lacy wanted to do it," I said.

"I see," Jeremiah said. "Good for them."

I was starting to feel uncomfortable and annoyed that my curiosity had gotten the best of me and put me in this position.

"I'll see you tomorrow, then," I said, turning to go.

"God bless you, Don," Jeremiah said as I walked away.

"And you," I said over my shoulder. *Where's the fire, Youngblood*? I thought.

✦ ✦ ✦

There was just the hint of darkness by the time I arrived back at the lake house. Presents were under the tree, and I saw no sign of Lacy and Biker.

"In here," Mary said.

"How was the mall?" I said as I entered the kitchen. Mary was alone.

"Uneventful. We spent some of your money."

"Where are the kids?"

"They're visiting high school friends. They'll be back later with pizza."

As soon as Mary was busy and not paying attention, I moved her presents from my SUV to under the tree. *Sneakiness is all.* After that, I busied myself doing prep for my meticulously prepared, much-demanded Caesar salad, which included making fresh croutons. I washed the lettuce and placed it in a salad spinner to remove excess water. Then I tore the lettuce into bite-sized pieces, put them in a gallon plastic bag, and placed the bag in the fridge. I cut up different varieties of bread into cubes, doused them lightly with butter and olive oil, sprinkled them with Italian seasoning, and baked them in the oven at 350 degrees. When the croutons acquired the proper brownness, I turned off the oven, opened the door, and let them cool while still in the oven. Doing it this way, I had found, made for the crispiest croutons known to man.

Mary opened a bottle of Bogle Phantom red as my reward, which of course was a joke, since she drank most of it. We were well into the red when Lacy and Biker returned with two pizzas. Once I tossed the Caesar salad and divided it up, we were ready to eat.

"I'd like to say grace," Mary said.

I was stunned but managed to say, "Sure."

"Sounds good," Lacy said.

"Let's hold hands," Mary said.

Mary was on my right and Lacy on my left in our little circle of four.

"Heavenly Father," Mary began, "let us be ever mindful of what this holiday season means, the birth of your son, savior of the world. We thank you for all our blessings: for family, for fellowship, and for this food. In your son's name we pray, amen."

Almost in unison, Lacy, Biker, and I said, "Amen."

"Thank you, Mom," Lacy said. "That was great."

"You're welcome," Mary said. "Eat."

I said nothing. I was speechless. This was a new Mary. We began to eat, and the mood lightened. The pizza and Caesar salad began to disappear.

"I went by the church today," I said.

"What for?" Mary said.

"I wanted to see the life-sized figurines that Jeremiah carved for the Nativity. They're astounding, as good in workmanship as you're ever going to see. He did most of the work with a chainsaw."

"Who is Jeremiah?" Lacy said.

"A very special and mysterious stranger who's new in town and seems to have a positive effect on all he meets," I said. "You'll see what I mean when you meet him. I'm sure he'll be at church tomorrow."

"He refurbished the deck and boathouse," Mary said. "They look spectacular."

"So, what time is church?" Lacy said.

"Eleven," Mary said. "Be there by ten forty-five."

"Biker is coming, too," Lacy said. "We'll be there."

✦ ✦ ✦

Lacy and Biker left. They were spending the night with some friends who had recently married. I didn't ask any questions. That ship had sailed. They were young adults and had to make their own decisions. Instead, I helped Mary clean up the kitchen and load the dishwasher. She was unusually quiet.

"Nice prayer tonight at dinner," I said. "What brought that on?"

"I don't know," Mary said. "It just felt right."

"I'm glad," I said. "It was special."

She said nothing, and we continued our work. I added dishwasher powder to the dispenser, closed the door, and pressed the start button. Mary shared the last of the red wine between us.

"Did you go to church as a child?"

"I did," I said. "You?"

"Yes," Mary said. "When did you stop going?"

"After my parents died." We had never had this discussion, and I was curious why we were having it now.

"Anger?"

"Lots," I said. "And guilt."

"For what?"

"For things I should have said and didn't."

"I can understand that," Mary said. "Which leads me to tell you that I love you with all my heart."

"And you know I feel the same way about you," I said.

"I do."

I sipped my wine and stared at my soulmate.

"Do you think our jobs make it hard for us to have faith in God?" Mary said.

The surprises just keep coming, I thought. I considered her question for a few moments before responding. "Probably. We certainly see the worst in people most of the time. And what we see is only a small sampling. It would be easy not to believe in God, but we need to realize that most people are good. The bad ones get all the attention. As we move forward, you'd hope the world becomes a better place, but that doesn't seem to be happening."

Mary took a drink of her wine. She set her glass down and moved to me and hugged me. I held her for a long time, wondering what was going on inside her head.

"What's on your mind?" I said.

"I'd like us to start going to church on a regular basis. Get involved and see where it leads. I feel I'm missing something. I'm hoping you feel the same way."

"I hadn't given it much thought," I said. "It's been okay. Whatever you want to do is fine with me. If you go, I'll go."

"I like that idea," Mary said. "I like it a lot."

24

Christmas Eve morning

We arrived at Mountain Center Methodist in time to take a good, long look at the bulletin. Lacy and Biker were waiting on us in the parking lot. In the vestibule, we studied the bulletin and made our decisions. We decided who would read which part and who would light the candles.

"I guess we should sit close to the front," Mary said.

"Lead the way," I said.

We were early enough to get four seats on the aisle five rows from the front. Biker entered the pew first, followed by Lacy, then Mary. I took the aisle seat. Pastor Adam came down to greet us. Mary

introduced Lacy and her fiancé, Biker McBride.
I smiled at that, since by definition fiancé implied an
engagement to be married. Had I missed something?

"I'll announce that the Youngbloods, Don, Mary,
and Lacy, will now come forward to light the Advent
candles and the Christ candle," Adam said. "Then
you-all come up and do the Advent liturgy and lighting. A butane stick lighter is on the table. I checked
to make sure it's working. There is also a book of
matches just in case. As soon as you finish, return to
your seats."

"Understood," Mary said.

Lacy and I nodded. Biker had the easy part. He
could stay in his seat. Pastor Adam moved away to
say hello to other parishioners.

"Fiancé?" I whispered in Mary's ear.

"Sounds better than boyfriend," she whispered
back.

"When is the wedding date?"

"Oh, shut up, smarty pants," Mary said.

By the time the organist started playing the pre-
lude, the church was nearly full, including the balcony.
The whole congregation stood and sang "Hark! The
Herald Angels Sing." The sound reverberated around
the sanctuary, and I had to admit it was impressive. We
sat back down, and Adam made a few announcements,
including times for the last Nativity performances. He
also gave a big thank you to Jeremiah James for his
part in all of it. There was a nice round of applause

for Jeremiah, who stood briefly, waved, and sat back down. I thought he looked embarrassed.

The moment came for our part in the service, and Pastor Adam made the announcement. I was none too thrilled about all of this, but the time for backing out had long since passed. I stood and took one step back as Mary and Lacy filed out. I followed them to the front of the church and up two steps near the altar to where the Advent candles were set up on a small table covered by a white lace tablecloth. I looked out over the congregation. The church was now full. Some younger people were standing near the back, no doubt having surrendered their seats to senior citizens. I felt like I was in a foreign country on a special assignment for which I was ill-equipped. I caught Jeremiah's eye. He was sitting on the front row. He smiled and nodded slightly, as if to say, *You'll be fine.*

I calmed myself, took a deep breath, and read aloud, "Rejoice at the good news! The Eternal Light has come into the world." I thought I sounded pretty good, and I relaxed a bit. While I read, Lacy, using the butane stick lighter, lit the four Advent candles. Then I read, "O God, now we light the candle of your Nativity!"

Lacy lit the center candle, the white Christ candle. Mary read, "With the company of heaven and with sounds of great joy, the Eternal Light of heaven comes to us. We celebrate this arrival. The son of God has been born among us."

Lacy read, "The prophet Isaiah foretold a time when those who walked in darkness would see a great light. The light would announce that a child had been born to all the world."

Mary read, "John proclaimed the great light to be Christ the Lord, the Word made flesh. This great light dwells among us, full of God's glory, a light of grace and truth. At Christ's Nativity, let us now rejoice." I saw tears in Mary's eyes. I stared at the floor.

The congregation read in unison, "God, our life and light, thank you for coming this night. Thank you for lighting heaven and earth with your splendor, shining in every corner of the world and in every corner of our hearts. Bring us eternal grace and peace, we pray, amen."

We returned to our seats as the congregation sang "The First Noel." The song engulfed the sanctuary, and I felt something pass through me that I cannot describe. I could feel the passion of the congregation, and I cannot deny that I was moved. Mary squeezed my hand. I dared not look at her, as I knew she was in an emotional moment.

After the service, we stood and waited as the church slowly emptied.

Jeremiah came from the front to greet us. "Nice job on the Advent liturgy, Youngbloods. I'm Jeremiah," he said, holding out his hand to Lacy. They shook.

"Nice to meet you," Lacy said. "This is Biker McBride, my fiancé."

Biker and Jeremiah shook hands.

"Nice to meet you Biker," Jeremiah said. "Are you a Harley man?"

"Yes, sir," Biker said.

"Me, too. We'll talk bikes in the near future."

"That would be great," Biker said.

"I'll see you tonight, Don," Jeremiah said.

"You will," I said.

Jeremiah nodded and moved away.

"Very nice job, all of you."

I turned around as Mary thanked Pastor Adam.

"Thank you," Lacy said.

"Enjoyed it," I said, just to say something different.

Pastor Adam patted me on the back and moved on.

"What's going on tonight?" Lacy said.

"A live Nativity," Mary said. "Don's a Wise Man."

"You're kidding," Lacy said.

I wish, I thought.

"This I've got to see," Lacy said.

"Me, too," Biker said.

I played it cool. I said nothing.

25

Christmas Eve

The last Nativity was at seven that evening. The night was dark and cold, with snow flurries. The players changed into their costumes in the choir room. The wardrobe committee—I'm not lying, there was one—made sure we looked presentable. I was the first Wise Man there and got the pick of the costumes. I chose the darkest one. Maybe no one would see me. The second Wise Man turned out to be Ted Booth, friend and bank president with an office one floor below mine in the Hamilton Building.

"I only agreed to do this because I heard you were one of the three Wise Men for the last show," Ted said.

"I think I said yes before I knew what I was doing," I said.

Ted laughed. "That sounds about right."

The third Wise Man showed up, and I couldn't believe my eyes. It was the trailer park manager, Rizzo. If I ever knew his first name, I had long forgotten it.

"Good to see you, Mr. Youngblood," he said. He offered his hand, so we shook. What was I to do? This couldn't be the same guy. "Nice job this morning with the candle lighting."

He was there? "Thank you," I said, looking over to Ted. "Do you know Ted Booth?"

"I don't," Rizzo said. "Anthony Rizzo. Pleased to meet you." Anthony and Ted shook hands. "I'm a little embarrassed doing this, but Jeremiah asked. He told me you were doing it, too, and before I knew it, I was saying yes."

"Jeremiah's hard to say no to," I said.

"You got that right," Rizzo said. "He's quite a guy."

We finished dressing and went out to take our places. The presentation played out pretty much the way it had on Friday night. I thought I'd be cold, but I wasn't. I thought the crowd would be smaller, but I was wrong about that, too. It was at least as big as the one on Friday night. I heard later that some people attended all three nights.

After it was over and I was back in my street clothes, I went outside where Mary, Lacy, and Biker were waiting.

"Good job, Don," Lacy said. "You looked really wise."

"I'm putting coal in your Christmas stocking," I said.

"Sure you are." She moved close, gave me a hug, and kissed me on the cheek. "Merry Christmas. We'll see you-all in the morning."

"Merry Christmas, Don," Biker said.

"And to you, Biker," I said. They headed toward their rental car.

I looked around for Jeremiah. He was helping take down the Nativity. I waved, and he walked over.

"Thanks for participating," he said.

"No problem," I said. "I actually enjoyed it, and I knew the other two guys."

"I know," he said. "I thought you'd be more comfortable if you did."

"The live Nativity was a nice thing for you to organize," Mary said. "So very many people enjoyed it."

"It was a blessing," Jeremiah said.

"Why don't you join us for dinner at the Fleet mansion tomorrow afternoon if you don't have other plans?" I said. "Mr. Fleet has a good chef, and I know the food and the fellowship will be worth it."

"That's sound wonderful," Jeremiah said. "I accept."

"We can pick you up," I said.

"No need," he said. "I'll drive."

"I'll text you directions," Mary said.

"No need." Jeremiah smiled. "I think I can find the Fleet mansion."

"You're right," I said. "It's not that hard to find."

"What's at the top of your Christmas list, Don?" Jeremiah said.

"World peace," I said quickly.

Jeremiah laughed. "That might take awhile."

"Okay," I said. "A white Christmas."

"I'll work on it," he said. "See you tomorrow." He turned and walked back to the Nativity.

"Why do I get the feeling that if we were to have Christmas dinner at a remote shack in the mountains, Jeremiah would know where it was?" Mary said.

"Because he would," I said.

✦ ✦ ✦

We went to the club for dinner. I was surprised the dining room was open. I later found out the staff was offered substantial bonuses for working Christmas Eve. They unanimously accepted. The deal included Christmas, and the day after, off with pay. The mood was cheerful and festive. The dining room was two-thirds full. We saw a lot of people we knew, including Ted Booth and his wife, Brenda. We were greeted by Jill, our favorite waitress, who had been at the club a long time. She was a short, above-average-looking blonde with a pleasant personality and a good memory. She took orders in her head. We ordered a bottle of red wine and told Jill we were in no hurry for dinner. Once the wine arrived, we shared the bottle and talked casually about a myriad of things, from Biker and Lacy to our new house.

About Biker and Lacy: "Do you know something about upcoming nuptials that I don't?"

"Only that it's going to happen after graduation," Mary said.

"Did Biker propose?"

"About like you did," Mary said.

I laughed. Mary had actually done the proposing. It took me about five seconds to say yes.

"So, Lacy pretty much told him they're getting married," I said.

"Pretty much."

"And he protested not at all."

"He said yes immediately. Much like you."

"What choice did he have?"

"None," Mary said.

"Much like me."

"Very much like you."

About the lake house: "It must be weird for you. It's the same house, but not really. How do you feel about it?"

"It's crazy," I said. "I miss the old house. I mean, it is the old house, in a way, but it isn't. I tell myself that my parents would approve, and I think they would, so I'm happy with it."

"I bet they'd approve of the dock and boathouse," Mary said.

"No doubt. My dad would be thrilled that I had that done."

We talked about other things as the evening drifted past nine o'clock and Jill took our orders. We both ordered fillets medium rare, baked potatoes, and steamed broccoli with melted white cheddar cheese. We set our jobs aside and talked about ghosts of Christmases past. We finished the bottle of wine as our food arrived.

"Another bottle?" Jill said.

"No," Mary said. "Bring me a glass of the same, and bring Don an Amber Bock."

"Be right back," Jill said. She hurried off as we began eating. The fillets were excellent, as always.

"What do you remember most about Christmas Eve before you were ten years old?" Mary said.

"That I had a hard time getting to sleep," I said. "I was hyper."

Mary laughed. "Weren't we all?"

Jill set our drinks down and went away.

"When did you stop believing in Santa Claus?" Mary said.

I tried to look surprised. "There's no Santa Claus? No way!"

This time, she giggled. The wine was having an effect. "You're too much. Answer the question, Cowboy."

"I'm not sure," I said. "I guess I was about six or seven. Big Bob told me. I played it cool, like I already knew. I kept it a secret from my parents that I knew. I figured the longer I believed in Santa, the better the presents would be. I liked finding stuff under the tree."

Our questions were fewer and more spaced out as we attacked our food.

"I didn't realize I was so hungry," Mary said.

"Me, too," I said. "This is really good."

In the lights outside, I could see light snow blowing. The wind was not allowing much of it to hit the ground. The forecast was for cold temperatures and snow flurries. My Apple watch showed it was twenty-nine degrees outside. The watch was a gift from Lacy last Christmas. She said I needed to get out of the Dark Ages. I had to admit, it was a lot more than just a watch.

When we finished, Mary said, "Dessert?"

"I'll share whatever you want."

I motioned for Jill, who had one eye on us. The dining room had cleared out, and only a few tables were occupied. She came immediately.

"Finished?"

"Yes," I said. "Great, as usual."

"Dessert?"

"One tiramisu and two spoons," Mary said.

"Back in a sec."

When we finished dessert, I signed the check and we got up to leave. I handed Mary a hundred-dollar bill. "Give this to Jill," I said. "Tell her Merry Christmas."

"Why don't you?"

"It's better if you give it to her," I said. "Woman to woman. Tell her it's from both of us."

As we walked out, Mary hung back and called to Jill. I kept on going. She caught up with me at the front door.

"That was a nice thing to do, Don," she said. "Jill was thrilled. She said to tell you Merry Christmas."

26

Christmas Eve, late

In the car, I got another surprise.

"Let's go to the late candlelight service," Mary said. "I haven't been to one since I was in high school. It starts in fifteen minutes. We can make it."

"Sure," I said without protest. Mary had really been captivated by the spirit of Christmas.

Ten minutes later, we walked through the front door of Mountain Center Methodist Church. We were handed a small white candle with a paper wax guard.

Pastor Adam was greeting people. "You're back," he said.

"We are," I said.

"This is the best crowd I've ever seen for the candlelight service," he said. "I wish I knew why."

I'll tell you someday, I thought. "Maybe it's the Nativity," I said.

"You could be right," he said, turning to greet someone else.

We found a seat. Five minutes later, the service started with the call to worship, a responsive reading, and "O Come, All Ye Faithful." During the hymn, Adam lit the four candles surrounding the Christ candle. Next was the opening prayer, also a responsive reading. The lights were dimmed, and Adam read from scripture and lit the Christ candle. The Christmas tree and the Advent wreaths on the windows were spotlighted. The effect was very theatrical. Adam then read the scripture about the birth of Jesus, and then Jeremiah appeared. Playing a twelve-string guitar, he sang "Mary, Did You Know?" His voice was clear as a bell, every note true and unwavering. A Broadway pro could not have done better. Adam read from Luke about the birth being announced to the shepherds, and the choir sang "O Holy Night." Adam continued with a prayer of confession and pardon, followed by the Lord's Prayer. After a short meditation about Jesus being the light of the world, the lights went dark except for the Advent candles and the Christ candle. Adam lit a small candle from the Christ candle, then lit the candle of the head usher, who in turn lit the candles of the other ushers. The ushers came down the aisles sharing the candle flame with the first person in each pew, who in turn lit the candle of the person next to them, and so on down the row. As they were lit, the darkness faded and the church glowed with candlelight. I was amazed at how much light the candles gave off.

"Go in peace as we sing 'Silent Night,' " Adam said.

Jeremiah started "Silent Night" with his twelve-string guitar, but it was soon drowned out by the soft singing of the congregation. We filed out silently. Just outside the front doors, we blew out our candles, dropped them in a basket, and headed silently for my SUV. We sat inside for a while absorbing the service, saying nothing.

"I love you, Don," Mary said. "Forever and always."

"I know," I said. "And I love you, Mary. But you already knew that."

"It's still nice to hear."

"It is," I said. I leaned over and kissed her. Tears were streaming down her face. "You okay?"

"I'm way better than okay. I've never been happier. Drive, Cowboy."

I started the SUV, and we drove back to the lake house in silence.

✦ ✦ ✦

We sat on our loveseat in front of the fire talking about memories. The gas logs looked real enough and put out some heat. No other lights were on in the room, making for a cozy atmosphere. Mary was practically in my lap.

"I think this is the best Christmas season I can ever remember," Mary said. "Why is that?"

"Well, for one thing, we've had more time to enjoy it," I said. "I'm not in the middle of a big case, and your caseload has been light."

"And we've reconnected with the way we were raised," Mary said.

"You mean church."

"That's certainly part of it," she said. "The whole town seems more into the spirit of Christmas than usual. Can one person make that much difference?"

"Apparently. Jeremiah started it and passed it on to a few others, and they passed it on, just like the flame we passed on tonight. A snowball effect. The live Nativity was the catalyst, I think."

"I was a little surprised that you invited Jeremiah to the Fleet Christmas dinner."

"I want Jeremiah to meet Joseph Fleet," I said.

"Why?"

I told Mary what Adam Church had told me about Jeremiah visiting the hospital. Then I told her about his phone call the next day after finding the patient much improved. I reminded her of Evan Smith's call about the miracle on the children's ward and the miraculous condition of the shooting victims.

"I saw Jeremiah kneel and say something to each gunshot victim as he touched them," I said. "I didn't think much about it at the time, but after talking to

Evan I'm wondering more and more who he is and what his abilities are."

"And you're just telling me all of this now?" Mary said.

"Things have been moving a little fast. I feel like I'm in the middle of a Hallmark movie."

We were quiet for a few moments.

"And you're hoping that Jeremiah might have a positive effect on Joseph Fleet's brain tumor," Mary said.

"It did cross my mind."

"That's really sweet, Don," Mary said. "You're just an ole softie, and you care a lot more about people than you let on. I am so proud of you."

27

Christmas Day

The next morning, I was in the kitchen having my first mug of coffee and staring out the window at the light snow falling. There was a dusting on the deck but not much on the ground. Still, it added another dimension to an already uniquely special Christmas season.

Mary was still sleeping. We had finally made it to bed and turned off the lights at two in the morning. I always got up at the same time, whether I had ten hours of sleep or the five I had just finished. The free-standing gas stove gave off enough heat to warm the kitchen, allowing the downstairs heating system to take a break.

Outside, the snowflakes were small but close together, and I couldn't see the end of the dock. Snow had not been forecast. I didn't even want to think what I was thinking. My cell phone snapped me out of it. Billy.

"Hey, Chief. Merry Christmas," I said.

"And to you also, Blood," he said. "Is it snowing over there?"

"Yes. Just started again. It's coming down pretty good."

"The road over the mountain is still open," Billy said. "If it closes, we would have to go through Maggie Valley and over to I-40. We might wait and come see you tomorrow or the next day. I'll keep an eye on things. I'll text you and let you know what we decide."

"Okay, Chief. Tell Maggie Merry Christmas."

"And tell Mary the same from me," Billy said. "I'll be in touch."

By the time I finished my conversation with Billy, the deck was covered in snow. It was beginning to look like a serious storm. I went to my home office, booted up my desktop computer, and pulled up

Doppler radar. The storm was a rotating circle about fifty miles in diameter with Mountain Center in the middle. It didn't seem to be moving, just spinning around. Cherokee, North Carolina, where Billy lived, seemed to be on the edge of the storm. I logged off Doppler and checked my email. Then I checked what was going on in the world of sports. I spent an hour online waiting for Mary to get up. I shut down and went back to the kitchen for another cup of coffee. Mary and I walked into the kitchen at the same time from different directions. She was still in her pajamas, robe, and house slippers, looking half awake.

"Merry Christmas," I said.

"And to you, my love," she said.

"Look outside."

"Wow," Mary said. "Where did that come from?"

"I don't know, but I've never seen anything like it on Doppler radar. It seems to be spinning around Mountain Center and not moving."

"I need coffee," Mary said, and proceeded to brew a mug of Dark Magic, using the Keurig.

My cell phone made the sound indicating I had a text message:

Right now I would say we are coming. Will let you know if that changes.

"Who was that?" Mary said.

"Billy."

"What about?"

"Just to let me know they're coming. He was worried about the roads."

Mary sat by the gas stove, drank coffee, and put a Christmas CD into our under-the-cabinet player. Nat King Cole started singing "I'll Be Home for Christmas." She finished her coffee, stood up, and stretched. "I've got to get dressed," she said. "Lacy and Biker will be here at ten o'clock to open presents."

I heard her thundering up the stairs, fully awake, the excitement of the day beginning to unfold. Then the phone started ringing. Mary's son, Jimmy, who lived in Nashville, was first to call. After that, Susan, Mary's daughter, called from California. Then Wanda Jones called from Las Vegas.

✦ ✦ ✦

A few minutes after ten o'clock, Lacy and Biker arrived. We sat down around the island in the kitchen and had coffee and freshly made cinnamon rolls hot out of the oven.

"How were the roads?" I said.

"Clear," Biker said. "Which was really weird. It's cold enough that snow should be sticking, but I guess the wind is blowing it off. It's gusty out there."

We moved to the living room, where Lacy played Santa Claus, handing out presents one by one as we opened them. An hour later, we were down to one, a gift for Mary from me. Lacy handed it to Mary.

"You might want to open that one later," I said.

"Like in the bedroom?" Lacy teased.

"I'll save it for later," Mary said.

"Mom!" Lacy said.

"And I'll show it to you before you go back to school," Mary said firmly.

"Okay," Lacy said. "Let's watch a Christmas movie."

So, we all went into the den, got cozy, and watched *Miracle on 34th Street.*

28

Christmas Day, evening

Almost everyone seemed to arrive at the Fleet mansion at the same time. T. Elbert pulled up in his Hummer H2 and Billy and Maggie in their Grand Cherokee. Jeremiah James rolled in on his Harley.

Roy Husky greeted us at the door.

"Nice to see you again, Roy," Jeremiah said.

"You, too," Roy said. "I hear you've been busy."

"Yes, I have," Jeremiah said. "Busy is good."

"You got that right," T. Elbert said, rolling up in his motorized wheelchair.

I introduced him to Jeremiah. As Jeremiah shook with T. Elbert, he put his other hand over the top of their two hands for a long moment. "It's a pleasure to meet you, T. Elbert," Jeremiah said. He said it as if he knew who T. Elbert was.

"Thank you," T. Elbert said.

"Follow me," Roy said.

Billy and Maggie trailed behind, just having parked their SUV. The group followed Roy down the hall, where we gathered in the living room for drinks and idle conversation. Christmas music played softly from a hidden source. I introduced Billy and Maggie to Jeremiah. Billy and Jeremiah exchanged a simple, quick handshake. Then Stanley Johns appeared, and I made another introduction.

Fifteen minutes later, Joseph made a grand entrance. "Welcome, everyone," he said with flair. "And to all of you, a very Merry Christmas!"

He seemed in an exceptionally good mood. I introduced him to Jeremiah, who shook his hand in much the same way he had with T. Elbert. "It's an honor to meet you, sir," Jeremiah said. "Thank you for including me in today's celebration."

"Well, I can't take credit for that," Joseph Fleet said. "Don was in charge of the guest list. But I'm glad you could join us."

We mingled awhile longer, and I noticed how Jeremiah worked the room, earnestly talking to each person a few minutes and then moving on. He hardly touched the glass of red wine in his hand. He drank wine like I did, a little sip every now and then.

Awhile later, Fleet's butler announced, "Dinner is served."

The group followed Joseph Fleet to the dining room, where a large, round table was set up with nine place settings. A long buffet table laden with food was on a far wall. *Nice seating arrangement*, I thought. Everyone could see each other. Jeremiah was on my right and Stanley Johns on my left. Clockwise after Stanley came Maggie, Roy, T. Elbert, Mary, Joseph Fleet, and Billy. We were evenly spaced. There were no place cards, and I found it interesting the way the group seated itself.

"I haven't seen you in a while, Stanley," I said. "How have you been?"

Stanley, a high school classmate, ex-hermit, and computer wizard, had helped me on some of my early cases by, reluctantly, doing some much-needed hacking. He was a round little man with dark, curly hair and a raspy voice, a gentle soul with the innocence of a child. I had introduced him to Joseph Fleet at a Fleet Thanksgiving bash, and they hit it off. Later, Fleet hired Stanley to prevent hackers from breaching Fleet Industries security systems. Stanley was now an important part of the Fleet operation. By the time he began working for Fleet, the FBI was doing my hacking, so I didn't need Stanley's services. The other major benefit of the Fleet job: it got Stanley out of his house.

"Busy," Stanley said. "What with Fleet Industries doing military work, we have to be extra cautious with our security. We've had a few attacks on our firewalls, but no one has been able to penetrate them. They never will, but that won't stop them from trying. It's a game. They're all trying to build a reputation. Like that group that hacked the gas pipeline. No reason for it, other than to prove they could do it. They have no conscience. They are bad people, Don." Stanley was starting to get upset.

"Well, I'm glad we have people like you around to stop them," I said. "Do you like what you're doing, Stanley?"

"I do. And if it wasn't for you, I wouldn't be doing it. Thank you for introducing me to Joseph Fleet, Don. I was a real hermit, and now I'm not."

"You made it happen, Stanley," I said. "Don't forget that."

At that moment, our conversation was halted by Joseph, who said, "Ladies and gentlemen, Jeremiah has agreed to offer our dinner prayer."

Suddenly, the room was completely quiet.

"Let us pray," Jeremiah said. "Heavenly Father, we give thanks for the love you sent to us so many years ago in the form of your son. We can feel that love in this room as we gather in fellowship to share this meal and celebrate the birth of Jesus. Help us all to understand the enormity of your gift. Bless this food and those who prepared it and we who are about to partake, amen."

A chorus of amens followed as we lifted our heads.

"Ladies, please go to the buffet now," Joseph Fleet said.

Mary and Maggie got to their feet and headed for the food. I noticed Jeremiah in quiet conversation with Billy, on his right.

"T. Elbert, please follow the ladies," Joseph Fleet said.

"My pleasure," T. Elbert said. He wheeled out from the table and fell in behind Mary.

"Gentlemen, please follow T. Elbert in any order you wish," Joseph said. "I'll be happy to lead the way."

I pushed away from the table, stood, and followed Joseph Fleet. The others fell in behind me, Billy and Jeremiah bringing up the rear. As I worked my way down the buffet, I took small portions so I could come back for seconds. I started with a salad from the salad bar, placed small portions of poached salmon and rice on my plate, and then made my way back to my seat. Jeremiah was close behind. His plate was considerably fuller.

"I hope that's not all you're eating," he said.

"My appetizer," I said. "The main course will come on my second trip."

"Smart," he said. "This is the best meal I've had in years. I'm going to take full advantage and pray I'm not being gluttonous."

We waited as the others returned. I noticed Billy's plate was full.

"*Bon appétit*," Joseph Fleet said, raising his fork.

The nine of us began eating.

"I've been meaning to tell you how much I like your artwork on Main Street," I said to Jeremiah. "You're a man of many talents."

"Thank you, but my talents, as are yours, are a gift from God. I thank God every day for them."

"Then you are truly blessed," I said, not sure exactly how to respond to that statement.

"I am," he said.

We ate in silence. It didn't take long for my plate to become empty. I excused myself and returned to the buffet. With a full plate, I returned to the table and sat down.

"Thank you for my Christmas present," I said to Jeremiah.

"You're welcome. A nice coincidence that I'm willing to take credit for, although I did offer up my snow prayer."

"You'll have to teach that one to me sometime."

"My pleasure," Jeremiah said.

We were silent for a moment, enjoying our food.

"I forgot to ask what's at the top of your Christmas list, Jeremiah," I said.

"I don't think I knew until late last night," he said. "And you and Mary are responsible."

"If it's within my power," I said, "it's yours."

"I think it is," he said.

"Tell me."

Very quietly, Jeremiah told me his Christmas wish.

"I should be able to do that," I said. "It might take a few days."

"No hurry," Jeremiah said. "I've been a long time waiting."

✦ ✦ ✦

After dinner, we retired back to the living room, where drinks were offered and served. I had my usual Baileys Irish Cream. I noticed Jeremiah also had Baileys. Mary finally made her way around to me. She was drinking Frangelico.

"Remind me to run about ten miles tomorrow," she said. "You can call me Miss Piggy."

"Remind me to go with you. I was an even bigger pig, but it was worth it."

"It certainly was," Mary said.

Mary looked gorgeous and festive in black slacks, a white sweater, and a red scarf. My Christmas wish was that we have many more years together.

✦ ✦ ✦

An hour later, Jeremiah was the first to leave. "I have an early morning," he said to Joseph Fleet. "I'm rebuilding a deck for a Mountain Center Methodist Church member. It's a three-day project, and I need to start early."

"So glad you could come," Joseph Fleet said.

"I cannot remember when I've had a better meal with better company," Jeremiah said, taking Joseph's hand in much the same way he had when first meeting him. "Thank you so much."

Jeremiah said his goodbyes to all of us, and the butler escorted him from the room. As usually happens when the first guest leaves, others took it as a cue. Stanley Johns was next.

"It was nice to see you, Don," he said. "Oscar is picking me up out front." Oscar, Joseph Fleet's chauffeur, worked with me from time to time.

"Take care, Stanley," I said. "And Merry Christmas."

"Merry Christmas to all," Stanley said as he walked away.

"Well, it's been fun," T. Elbert said to the group. "But it's way past my bedtime. Joseph, you sure know how to throw a party. Thanks for having me."

"Thanks for coming," Joseph Fleet said. "Always a pleasure."

"Good night, everyone," T. Elbert said as he wheeled toward the door.

"Ready?" I said to Mary.

"Ready," she said.

We said our goodbyes. Billy agreed to meet me for breakfast at the Mountain Center Diner. He and Maggie were staying over at the Fleet mansion, as they often did after Fleet events. The butler escorted us to the front door. We knew the way, of course, but it was his job, and he would have been offended if we didn't let him. *Protocol is all.*

29

The day after Christmas

Midmorning the next day, I met Billy at the Mountain Center Diner. The crowd was light. Many businesses were closed and would open sporadically through the first of the year. Mountain Center would be in full swing again. I arrived first through the back door. Five minutes later, Billy came through the front. More than one pair of eyes looked up at the six-foot-six Cherokee. He moved through the diner like a big cat and sat down across from me.

"Sleep well, Chief?"

"Slept great," he said. "When I finally got to sleep." He smiled.

"Then you must be pretty hungry."

"Starved," Billy said.

As if on cue, Doris arrived with coffee and to take our orders. First, she had to fuss over Billy. Anytime Billy was in the Mountain Center Diner, it was an event.

"Where is Maggie?" I asked.

"Still sleeping," Billy said.

"Mary, too."

He raised his mug and took a drink of coffee. "Nice gathering last night. Great food."

"It was," I said. "What did you think of Jeremiah James?"

"He gives off a vibe and has the disposition of a Cherokee medicine man," Billy said. "He has a gentle, thoughtful spirit that makes you want to listen to what he has to say, yet he's a bit guarded."

"Christmas Eve, he asked me what I wanted for Christmas. I told him a white Christmas."

"And you got one," Billy said.

"I did. And it was not in the forecast."

"So, you think he can control the weather?"

"Not really, but it is kind of otherworldly."

"There's your problem," Billy said. "You always need to have answers for everything."

"I guess," I said.

"I know," Billy said.

I didn't tell Billy about Jeremiah's request. I was treating that as confidential.

twelve Native American tribes. Being from a tribe myself, I was always interested in that."

"Name the twelve Native American tribes you memorized."

"Why?"

"Because I'm interested to see which twelve you picked, and how many I've heard of," I said. "I know there's a whole lot more than twelve."

"Actually, there are over five hundred Native American tribes in the United States. Almost half of those are in Alaska."

Breakfast was disappearing slowly. Billy was talking much more than usual. I normally carried our conversations. I had stumbled upon an old memory of his. Billy rarely shared the past, and I was going to take full advantage.

"So, who did you pick?"

"Cherokee, of course," Billy said. "The other eleven I picked were Apache, Blackfoot, Chickasaw, Chippewa, Choctaw, Iroquois, Muscogee, Navajo, Pueblo, Shawnee, and Sioux."

"Don't think I've ever heard of the Muscogee tribe," I said. "I've heard of the others. Is the Cherokee tribe the largest?"

"No," Billy said. "We're the second largest, by a wide margin over the Sioux. The Navajo tribe is the largest, but not by a lot."

"Interesting," I said. "You never cease to amaze me, Chief."

✦ ✦ ✦

Walking down the alley to the office after breakfast, I noticed the day had warmed nicely. I smiled. Jeremiah did say he was building an outdoor deck. He seemed to have an in with the weather gods. I climbed the back stairs and came out on the second floor close to my outer office door. The floor was eerily quiet. All the offices were closed. I had given Gretchen and Rhonda the week off. We officially reopened the day after New Year's.

At my desk, I texted Mary,

Are you up?

No response. I checked the answering machine for messages. None. I went online and looked at the Dow. Not much change. I shut down and was ready to leave when my cell phone rang: Mary.

"Hey," I answered.

"Hey yourself. I'm up with coffee in hand. How was breakfast?"

"Fine," I said.

"Learn anything?"

"Billy thinks Jeremiah acts very much like a Cherokee medicine man. Other than that, not much."

"That's interesting. We'll talk more tonight. Right now, I have to shower and get dressed. I promised Big Bob I'd be in by noon. See you tonight."

"Stay alert," I said.

"Always," she said. "Love you."

"Love you, too," I said.

✦ ✦ ✦

On my way back to the condo, I drove by the church. The life-sized Nativity was still up. A sign said, **Nativity will remain available for viewing through New Year's Day.** The Christmas spirit is staying a little longer this year in Mountain Center, I thought. I parked and stared at the scene, wondering how one man could make such a difference in our town. Then I thought, Why not? One man made a lot of difference for the world.

30

The next two days

Tuesday morning, Lacy and Biker came by the condo to say goodbye.

"We'll go skiing during your winter break," I said. "I'll let you know where. My treat."

"I'll really miss you-all," Mary said. "It was great having you around."

"We'll see you soon enough," Lacy said.

We exchanged hugs all around, and then they were gone. The tough cop had tears in her eyes. I gave her a hug and said nothing.

"Got to go," Mary said without making eye contact. "See you tonight."

She was out the door before I could utter a response. Having nothing better to do, I took the dogs and went to the lake house. I put a lot of effort into finding things to keep myself busy. I did some cleaning, rearranged bookshelves, and used the leaf blower to chase away random leaves that had gathered on both decks. The temperature seemed ten degrees colder than in town, and the wind was blowing at a decent clip. After an hour, I brought the dogs, who had been in the side yard, back into the warm confines of the new house. We returned to Mountain Center in time to meet Mary for dinner at the condo.

✦ ✦ ✦

Wednesday, I went to the office and cleaned out files, throwing out unneeded paperwork. None of it had to be done. It was busywork, pure and simple. I was bored.

Around lunchtime, I heard the outer office door open and shut.

"Don, are you here?"

I knew the voice and was surprised by it. He had never been in my office, although I had visited his on more than one occasion.

"In here," I called. "Come on back."

Dr. Evan Smith walked in. He was carrying a large envelope in his left hand.

"Evan, this is a surprise," I said. "Have a seat."

He sat in the oversized chair directly in front of my desk.

"Is everything okay?"

"Everything is fine," Evan said. "I'm trying to satisfy my curiosity."

"About what?"

"About everything that's going on at the hospital."

"There's more than you told me?"

"There is. And I absolutely cannot explain it medically."

"Tell me," I said.

"First, all the gunshot victims were home for Christmas," he said. "They healed about twice as fast as we expected. Then there's the woman who should be dead." He held up the envelope.

"The one with a bullet behind her heart," I said.

"Yes. With one small change."

From the envelope, he removed two x-rays. He handed me one of them. "Taken when she came into the hospital," he said. "The solid white mass is the bullet." He handed me the second x-ray. "Taken this morning. Twice." There was no solid white mass.

"Where's the bullet?"

"You tell me," Evan Smith said.

I thought for a moment. "Dissolved?"

"Apparently. I've never heard of such a thing. I'm going to research it and see if I can find anything similar. I'm tempted to write this one up for a medical journal, but no one would believe it. You have any thoughts?"

"Has to be something medical science is missing," I said.

"But what?"

"I don't know. You're the doctor. Test her blood to see if anything is different. The bullet didn't just vanish. Something in her body ate that bullet."

"The blood test is a good idea," he said. "I'll do that. Also, she told me one other thing I found strange."

"What's that?"

"She said a man knelt down beside her and touched her and told her she was going to be okay."

"What man?" I said, knowing full well it was Jeremiah.

"She can't remember," Evan Smith said.

We both sat silently. I wasn't about to say what I was thinking. Finally, I said, "Guardian angel?"

"Apparently," Evan Smith said. "I have no other explanation."

✦ ✦ ✦

That night, I told Mary about my conversation with Evan Smith.

"The bullet just vanished?" Mary said, incredulous.

"Gone, goodbye," I said.

"So, by some miracle, the bullet dissolved. It has to be biological. Something in her body. Something rare."

"Probably. But a flat-out miracle nonetheless."

"Like the Yeti that saved your life," Mary said.

My coffee-filled Yeti had gotten in the way of a sniper's bullet almost a year ago. If it hadn't, I might be dead. Blind luck or divine intervention? That was the question. I was leaning toward divine intervention.

"Not quite like that," I said. "But in the ballpark."

"You need a professional opinion," Mary said.

"Who do you suggest?"

"Father John."

I pointed my index finger at her. "That's not a bad idea."

31

Four days after Christmas

Father John Kelly was a Catholic priest I had met while working on the Crane case, pursuing the murderer of Walter Crane, one of a group of soldiers known as the Southside Seven. Father John, also one of the seven, had a congregation in Evanston, Illinois. He had been there since I met him. We talked occasionally, maybe twice a year. Early that Friday, I dialed his cell phone.

"Don," he answered. "Happy holidays."

Caller ID leaves no surprises. "And to you, Father John," I said.

"Is everything okay?"

"Yes, it is. I called because we haven't talked in a while and I want to get your take on something."

"Are you working a case?"

"Not really, but I do have a mystery man I want to tell you about. The telling of it will take awhile."

"I like it already," Father John said. "Take all the time you need. My life can get pretty boring doing the day-to-day."

"His name is Jeremiah," I began.

"One of the four major prophets of the Old Testament," Father John interjected. "Sometimes called 'the Weeping Prophet.' "

"If you say so."

"Sorry," he said. "I got a little carried away there. Can't help showing off from time to time. Please continue. I'll try not to interrupt."

"I was in a rather notorious bar and grill . . . ," I began.

". . . And that's what I know so far," I said when I finished my story twenty minutes later.

There was a moment of silence on the other end. "That's quite a story, Don," Father John said. "If it hadn't come from you, I'd be skeptical. But you're the most observant, clear-headed person I know, so I'm sure your story isn't exaggerated. Jeremiah sounds like a godsend, a wonderful human being, if he is a human being."

"What else could he be?"

"It's possible he could be an angel," Father John said. "The general consensus is that angels do not take human form—or if they do, only briefly. But there is much we don't know about them. Angels are mentioned over two hundred times in scripture. You may have encountered one in Jeremiah. Whoever or whatever he is, he has definitely been chosen by God."

"So, you believe this is possible, that he could be an angel?"

Keith Donnelly

"Anything is possible where God is concerned," Father John said. "What has he said to you about who he is?"

"He's been vague," I said. "He implied that he'll be leaving soon and will answer all my questions."

"Then you need to be patient and wait. If he said he'll answer your questions, then I'm sure he will."

"I'll be patient, Father," I said. "Thank you for the counsel."

"And please, Don, after this is over, call me. I would very much like to know what Jeremiah tells you."

"I will, Father John," I said. "I promise."

32

New Year's Eve

Saturday, I watched football at the lake house. Mary had volunteered to work so another officer could be with his pregnant wife. I still had those occasions when I enjoyed being by myself. Mary and I spent a lot of time together, and I always thought it was healthy to have some time apart. By the time she arrived at the lake house Saturday afternoon, I was starting to miss her. I kept that to myself. *Toughness is all.*

Sunday, we were back in church for the eleven o'clock traditional service. We didn't even discuss it, we just got ready and went. Adam Church presided over the service, and his sermon was about looking ahead with resolution and anticipation for the coming year. Jeremiah played his twelve-string guitar and sang "'Til the Season Comes Round Again." It sounded like a goodbye to me.

"I think his song means he's leaving," Mary whispered in my ear.

"Exactly what I was thinking," I said.

To close the service, Jeremiah sang "Pray for Me," written by Michael W. Smith. The song started, "Here is where the road divides," and the chorus concluded,

Pray for me and I'll pray for you
Pray that we will keep the common ground
Won't you pray for me and I'll pray for you
And one day love will bring us back around again

There was no doubt in my mind that Jeremiah was saying goodbye to everyone present.

✦ ✦ ✦

After the service, many of the parishioners mingled in the foyer to greet each other. At one point, I found myself alone on the opposite side from Mary. Jeremiah slipped up beside me.

"Glad to see you here, Don," he said.

"You're leaving," I said.

"I figured you'd pick up on that."

"Who else knows?"

"No one, unless they've deduced it."

"I'm sorry you have to leave."

"Me, too," Jeremiah said. "But I do, and I promised you that I'd answer all your questions, so let's meet tomorrow morning, and I'll do that."

"Coffee, my office," I said. "I have a Christmas present for you."

"Wonderful," he said. "Eight o'clock okay?"

"Perfect," I said. "I'll text you the entry code to the back door. Come up the stairs to the second floor and go left. You can't miss it. I'll leave the door open."

"See you then," Jeremiah said. He slipped away into the crowd.

33

New Year's Day

Early on New Year's Day, I drove from the lake house to my Mountain Center office in the Hamilton Building. Traffic was nonexistent. I felt like I was in a sci-fi movie where I was one of the few people left on the planet. Mary and I had spent New Year's Eve at the lake house. I grilled filet mignon, baked potatoes in the oven, and tossed a Caesar salad. The weather had turned colder, so we set up the bistro table and ate in front of the fireplace, sharing a bottle of Cabernet Sauvignon.

I went up the back stairs of my building at seven forty-five carrying an assortment of muffins Mary had made: blueberry, bran, corn, and chocolate chip. I turned on some lights, got two mugs out of the cabinet, and set out an assortment of muffins and K-Cups on the conference table.

At exactly eight o'clock, Jeremiah James walked through the outer office door. He smiled. "Good morning."

"And to you," I said. "Coffee?"

"Absolutely," he said.

"Pick your poison."

He chose a K-Cup of Dunkin' Donuts regular blend. I popped it in the Keurig and brewed it into a mug. Then I repeated the action for myself and added cream and sugar. We sat and took that first, best sip. Jeremiah nodded.

"Muffin?"

"Sure," he said. "Corn would be good."

I took a corn muffin and a blueberry muffin and put them in the microwave for twenty seconds.

Thirty seconds later, we were eating warm muffins and drinking hot coffee.

"Perfect," he said.

"You're welcome to another muffin," I said.

"I might just do that later. You're a patient man, Don. Ask your questions. You might want to record this for Mary or anyone else you think you need to play it for."

"You don't mind?"

"No, I don't mind. I know you'll be discreet."

I pulled a recorder from my desk, pressed the record button, and got right to it. "What did you say to the shooter at the mall? It sounded like something in Hebrew."

"Hebrew?" he said. "I thought I was speaking English. I said, 'Demon, in the name of Jesus Christ, be gone.' I cannot tell you why I said that. It just came out of my mouth."

"Who are you, really?"

"Jeremiah James," he said.

"Date of birth?"

"April 28, 1944."

"That would make you seventy-seven years old."

"It would," Jeremiah said.

"That's not possible."

"Actually, Don, anything is possible through God if you believe and have faith. I admit, my aging is hard to explain."

I paused for a moment, almost afraid to ask the next question. "This is going to sound crazy, but are you an angel?"

"No," he said. "Of that, I am sure. I'm just a man God has chosen to bestow with some unique gifts, a man who doesn't age like everyone else."

"Did you die in a fall when you were twenty years old?"

He paused and smiled. "You did some homework. I did have a fall, yes. I don't know if I was dead or not. I thought I was dead, but obviously I'm alive."

"Could you explain that, please?"

"I'll try," he said. "I remember climbing, and I remember falling. I remember thinking, *Lord, this is not the way I want to die.* I do not remember hitting the ground. The next thing I remember is being pulled toward a bright light. Then a voice said, 'It is not your time, Jeremiah. There is much more for you to do.' The next thing I remember is that it was morning and I was back inside my van. I wasn't hurt. No bumps, no bruises, no cuts, nothing wrong. I thought I had dreamed it until I saw the Santa Fe newspaper. Then I was really confused."

"Why didn't you contact the authorities to let them know you were alive?"

"I didn't want the publicity," Jeremiah said. "You can imagine the headline: 'Miracle Man Survives Death Fall without a Scratch.' They would have wanted to put me in a cage and study me like a guinea pig. I had no next of kin to notify, so I thought I'd keep my mouth shut and let them think they had lost my body."

I could relate to his decision. On more than one occasion, I had to fend off the press until they got tired of pursuing me.

"A lot of this is going to sound crazy," Jeremiah said, "but I think you'll understand when I'm finished. Anyway, the next night, I had a dream. An angel appeared to me and told me to go to Durango, Colorado. He said, 'There, you will find work.' I dismissed it as only a dream, and the next day I went for a hike, a safe one. That night, I had the exact same dream. I woke the next day disturbed by it. I had to get out of there. I packed up and headed to Albuquerque to see the hot-air balloons. The third night was something more than a dream. The angel said, 'Jeremiah, do not ignore me for a third time. Hasten thee to Durango. There, you will find your destiny.' The dream was so vivid and real. Later, I was convinced it was a visitation by an angel, that he was in the room with me. There are over a hundred references to angelic visitations in scripture.

"So, I did as the angel instructed and drove to Durango the next day. I bought a local newspaper and saw an ad for a carpenter's assistant. I had worked two summers building houses. I answered the ad and got the job, partly because I had a van and my own tools. I was there until the weather turned cold and I was no longer needed. Then I had another dream that told me where to go next. It's been like that ever since. I have dreams that tell me when it's time to move on, and where to go. Through the years, the dreams have been more like dreams, not nearly as real as the visitation."

"Why do you think you were sent to Durango?"

"I'm not entirely sure, but the man I worked for had cancer," Jeremiah said. "A godly man. He and his family had prayed every day for healing. When I left, he was cancer-free. I think I was sent to heal this man, but I have no idea how I did it. As the years went by, it became clear to me that I had the gift of healing, but I wasn't sure how it worked. And as I look back, there was an incident when I was in high school that might have given me a clue."

"Do your dreams ever tell you to go and heal someone specifically?"

"No," Jeremiah said. "The angel in my dreams only tells me when it's time to go, and where to go."

"Is it always the same angel?"

"Yes."

"Does he have a name?"

"I'm sure he does, but I don't know it. Very few angels are named in the Bible. Gabriel and Michael are the most well-known, along with Lucifer, who, of course, is the fallen angel, Satan."

"Interesting," I said. "Have you ever tried to question this angel?"

"Once," Jeremiah said. "You have to understand, I was in such awe of this creature that I couldn't speak. Finally, after maybe his tenth visit, I found my voice in my dream and asked, 'Why me?' His response was, 'Why not you? You should rejoice that you have been chosen.' That was the one and only time I tried to question him."

"So, this has been your life for fifty-some years?"

"Yes. I've become so used to traveling and meeting new people that I don't think I could ever really settle down. I always find work, I always meet wonderful people, and I'm always provided for. I never want for anything."

I said nothing for a moment or two. I was processing the unbelievable. "More coffee?"

"Please," Jeremiah said.

"Another muffin?"

"I'll try the chocolate chip."

I made another round of coffee and warmed two more muffins, both chocolate chip. All the time, my mind was in chaos. What I was hearing was too fantastic to process.

"Why haven't you aged?"

"I do age," Jeremiah said, "just not like normal people. As best I can figure, I age about half as fast, maybe a little less. I must have started aging less in high school or soon after. I figure I might live to be a hundred and twenty or more. Another good reason not to stay in one place too long."

"Did you tell anyone you were still alive?"

"A few friends at the time who I didn't want to worry," he said. "I told them the article was a mix-up, that I had spent some time in the hospital but was okay. I haven't stayed in touch with them, for obvious reasons."

"So, no next of kin anywhere?"

"None that I know of. My parents were killed in a car accident right before I graduated high school. I think that's why I was so reckless until the fall. I was taking chances—riding fast on my motorcycle, making dangerous climbs without the proper safety equipment, things like that. I have some money in the bank from my parents' accident insurance that I rarely touch. I sold the house before I moved out west. I like to earn money as I go from place to place. I enjoy working and meeting new people."

"I know what it's like to lose your parents while you're in high school," I said.

"I know you do," Jeremiah said.

I drank coffee and stared out the window. I hated to think about the death of my parents. I suppressed the memory with a passion. Jeremiah waited patiently.

"How many people have you healed?"

"I have no idea," Jeremiah said. "I'm rarely around long enough to find out the end result. Like Johnny Appleseed, planting seeds but never staying around long enough to see what happens. All I know is that if I'm around sick or injured people, they seem to heal, or at least improve. If I touch them, better yet. I really don't understand how any of it works."

My head was spinning. I had a thousand questions that I couldn't untangle. "Why did you come to Mountain Center?"

"To see you," Jeremiah said.

"Me? Why?"

"To help you find your faith, Don. To help you put aside your guilt. To let you know that you're special, a protector in God's army. To tell you to keep fighting for good and opposing evil and injustice."

"I don't understand," I said, feeling off-balance.

"You were chosen, Don. Have you ever wondered why you've been put in the position to save so many lives? You were dead once yourself and were sent back, remember?"

"No, I don't."

"In Las Vegas," he said. "In the hospital, you told Mary you had a dream that you saw your parents."

I stared at him. How could he know so much? I felt a chill pass through me as I remembered the dream I had dismissed years ago.

"My mother told me to go back, that it wasn't my time. I never told that to anyone. How did you know?"

"I don't know," Jeremiah said. "Sometimes, I know things that are like old memories from someone else. I don't know how, they're just there."

I was having a hard time keeping up. Maybe I was dreaming now.

"And the bullet that was stopped by the Yeti," he said, "that wasn't blind luck. You were, and are, being protected. You have much work left to do. The battle between good and evil will not stop until the end of the age. You and Mary will live long and happy lives together and keep many people from harm."

I sat in silence. Eli Wirkus, the sniper who tried to kill me, believed the reason he failed was because I was protected by angels. At the time, I dismissed the idea. Now, I wasn't so sure.

All the questions I wanted to ask faded away like smoke on a strong wind. My mind was blank. We were silent, drinking our coffee and eating our muffins. I stopped the tape recorder.

"I must go," Jeremiah said. "Please tell Mary and the others I said goodbye."

"I will. What's your next stop?"

"You tell me," he said. "The angel came to me in a dream last night and said I was to go where you sent me."

Me tell him? "Oh," I said. "I understand. I almost forgot." I handed him an envelope lying on my desk. It contained an address and some cash.

He peeked inside. "What is this?"

"Your destination and a little traveling money. You'll need it. You're going a long way. Text me when you can. I'll be interested in your progress and when you arrive."

Jeremiah nodded. He extended his hand, and I took it. He held it longer than normal. "May God bless you and keep you," he said. "And may his light shine upon you always."

"And you," I said.

He turned and walked out of my office. I heard the outer office door open and shut. I felt a sadness come over me. I had gotten used to having Jeremiah around. I didn't want him to leave, but part of me understood that he must. I prayed that it wasn't the last time I would see Jeremiah James.

✦ ✦ ✦

I arrived at the lake house late that afternoon to find my lovely wife and a bottle of red wine waiting for me in the kitchen. I came in, sat down at the island, and placed the tape recorder in front of me. Mary smiled but said nothing. She poured wine for both of us, sat across from me, and raised her glass. We touched glasses in silence and took our first drink in unison. She looked down at the tape recorder, then up at me.

"What's this?"

"Something that's going to give new meaning to our lives," I said.

"Really?"

I nodded.

"Play it," she said.

I pressed the play button and heard myself say, "What did you say to the shooter at the mall?"

By the time the tape finished, tears were streaming down Mary's face. "I'm stunned," she said. "I don't know what to say. It's unbelievable, yet I believe everything Jeremiah says."

"As do I."

"You tried to tell me about your dream in Vegas," Mary said. "About your parents. I told you it was probably the drugs, and you never mentioned it again. Why?"

"There was a lot going on, and the dream faded into the background. I thought you were right, that it probably was the drugs."

"And now?"

"I think it was real," I said.

We sat in silence as my last statement hung in the air.

"What do we do now?" Mary said.

"Keep doing what we're doing and hope we can make a difference. I need to find my next big case."

PART TWO

34

New Year's Day and beyond

*D*on was right, Jeremiah thought after looking at the address he had been given. *I do have a long way to go.*

Driving his van with his motorcycle trailing behind it, Jeremiah departed Mountain Center as soon as he left Donald Youngblood's office. He programmed the address into his GPS. His first stop was Indianapolis, Indiana. Normally, he would find a nice campground and sleep in his van. In cold weather, he usually found a decent hotel or motel. He spent his first night in a Hampton Inn off I-65. He picked up a Subway sandwich, a bag of chips, and a Diet Coke for dinner and settled in to watch TV. Before turning in for the night, he texted Donald Youngblood:

Arrived in Indianapolis. Easy trip. Hello to Mary. Blessings!

A few minutes later, Don texted back:

Thanks for the info. Safe travels.

Jeremiah read for a while, said his nighttime prayers, then turned out his bedside lamp and went to sleep.

The next day, Tuesday, he was awake early. He said his morning prayers and went to the fitness center. He worked out for forty-five minutes. He didn't often pay for a hotel, so he intended to take full advantage of everything it had to offer. He showered, packed, and went to the dining room for the free breakfast. Thirty minutes later, he was on the road.

Traffic that day was moderate, and Jeremiah made good time. While he drove, he listened to a book on his CD player. The book made the time pass faster. Late that afternoon, he checked in to the Cambria Suites in Madison, Wisconsin. The Cambria was in the rolling countryside near a large pond not far from the interstate. He liked the location.

For dinner, he ate at the hotel bistro, then returned to his room to check the weather on his laptop. He didn't want to unknowingly drive into a snowstorm. The weather for tomorrow's leg of his long trip looked good. He hoped Don's information was accurate. He would hate to drive almost two thousand miles to find out it wasn't. That reminded him to text Don:

Arrived in Madison, Wisconsin. Good trip. Hello to Mary. Blessings!

Almost immediately, he received a reply:

Good to hear. Have a good night's sleep. Safe travels.

He said his nighttime prayers, then read for an hour. His book was getting good. Finally, no longer able to keep his eyes open, he gave up and turned out the light.

Wednesday was colder and overcast. Jeremiah was up early for his morning prayer time and a workout in the well-equipped fitness center. Forty-five minutes later, he was in the shower. He dressed, packed, and put everything in the van. Then he went to the bistro for breakfast. A half-hour later, he was rolling.

Traffic was light except around the Twin Cities. Occasionally, he encountered windblown snow flurries, but nothing significant enough to slow him down. He drove and listened to his audiobook. Late in the afternoon as he put the finishing touches on a five-hundred-mile day, he pulled into the check-in parking space of the Fargo Residence Inn. After he checked in to a studio suite, Jeremiah went to a nearby restaurant, Old Chicago Pizza. He ordered a turkey-bacon club sandwich, fries, and a draft. The crowd was light and the waitress attentive.

"You live around here?" she asked as she brought his order. Her nametag said she was Millie. Millie was a trim, attractive blonde with a ponytail. She reminded him a little of Mary Youngblood, although not as tall.

"Just passing through, Millie," he said. "Leaving in the morning."

"Too bad."

Jeremiah smiled and said nothing.

"Enjoy," she said, and walked away.

Jeremiah ate slowly, enjoying every bite. While he ate, he texted Donald Youngblood:

In Fargo, ND. Easy trip so far. Hello to Mary. Blessings.

He didn't hear back from Don. He paid the bill and said goodbye to Millie.

As he turned to go, Millie said, "What's your name?"

"Jeremiah."

"Jeremiah," she said. "It fits. Have a nice life, Jeremiah."

"You, too, Millie."

Thursday morning, Jeremiah skipped the free breakfast at the Residence Inn. The weather didn't look good, and he wanted to get moving. He prepared a coffee to go. He would grab a bite later, he decided. On his phone, he saw a text from Don:

Storm moving your way. Be careful. Safe travels.

Back on the road, he headed north toward Canada. It was a cloudy, overcast day with snow in the forecast.

Jeremiah knew he would be fine, but the forecast made him nervous. He drove north on Interstate 29. A little over two hours later, he crossed the Canadian border at Huron City and entered the province of Manitoba. He proceeded north on Canada Highway 75 and ran into an unexpected blinding snowstorm. Youngblood was right.

35

Very early January

The spirit of Christmas was slow to depart Mountain Center. The normal routine was returning at a snail's pace. Decorations were taken down, but the storefront windows maintained the artwork of Jeremiah James. The Nativity in front of Mountain Center Methodist Church was finally disassembled and carefully packed away for next Christmas. I was part of the crew that did the heavy lifting. I still marveled at Jeremiah's craftsmanship.

Thursday morning, I sat on T. Elbert's front porch with Roy drinking coffee and eating pastry from the chef at the Fleet mansion. Specifically, I was working on a cheese Danish, trying to eat slowly so I could savor it, but not having much success.

"I think I'm suffering from post-Christmas depression," T. Elbert said. "This Christmas season was really special. I'm sorry it had to end."

"I'm feeling a little down myself," I said.

"No time to dwell on that," Roy said. "I have a business to run."

"Heard from Jeremiah?" T. Elbert said in my direction.

"He's been updating me on his progress," I said. "I expect to hear from him tonight. There's a big storm the way he's headed. He might get caught in it."

"I hope he'll be okay," T. Elbert said. "I really liked that guy."

"He will be," I said.

We were quiet for a while. I thought about all that had happened since Roy and I met Jeremiah James at the Bloody Duck right after Thanksgiving. It seemed like a lifetime ago, and yesterday at the same time.

"I need to tell you two something," T. Elbert said.

I heard the seriousness in his voice, and a wave of fear passed through me. I wasn't ready for any bad news.

"I'm almost afraid to share this for fear it was my imagination," T. Elbert said.

"Out with it," Roy said.

"My foot woke me up last night," T. Elbert said. "It was itching. I scratched it, and the itch went away. Then I went back to sleep without realizing the significance. When I woke up this morning and remembered last night, I started rubbing my foot, and I could swear I felt something. I'm scared to death my mind is playing tricks on me."

Jeremiah, I thought. "Which foot?" I said.

"My left foot," T. Elbert said.

T. Elbert had a blanket in his lap that covered his legs. I removed the blanket and handed it to Roy.

"Let's do a little test," I said. I scooted my chair in front of T. Elbert, raised his left leg, and placed it in my lap. I removed his shoe and sock. "Pull your hat down over your face."

T. Elbert pulled his hat down.

I picked up a fork that was lying on the table. "Okay, concentrate. I'm going to poke around. Let's see if you feel anything. Ready?"

"Okay," T. Elbert said.

"Feel that?" I said without touching him.

"No," he said.

I firmly poked his thigh and then his calf. "Anything?"

"No."

Then I poked the bottom of his foot.

"Ouch!" T. Elbert said. He raised his hat and looked at me wide-eyed. "I felt that, Donald! I felt that!" He looked at Roy. "I felt that!"

Roy's eyes were watering. I poked T. Elbert again in a different spot on his foot.

"Ouch!" he said. "Take it easy, Donald."

I laughed. Then Roy laughed. And then we were all laughing. The laughter was born not from humor, but from joy, from thanksgiving, from celebration, from witnessing a miracle.

36

The Thursday after New Year's

Later that same morning, Jeremiah was driving in a blizzard as he headed farther north into Canada. He was following an eighteen-wheeler that was moving slowly but steadily through the howling storm. The eighteen-wheeler exited at Provincial Road 201 in Letellier, Manitoba. Jeremiah followed and found himself in the parking lot of Barnay's Restaurant and Lounge, an obvious favorite of truckers, given the number of rigs in the lot.

He fought his way through the storm carrying his backpack. Once inside, he found an out-of-the-way table and ordered breakfast. He pulled up Doppler radar on his cell phone to get an idea how big an area the storm covered. It was large but was moving east at a decent clip. All he could do was wait it out. He ordered a full breakfast and ate every bite.

Later, a man who seemed to be leaving stopped at his table. "That your van pulling the motorcycle?"

"Yes, it is," Jeremiah said.

"I'm the guy driving the eighteen-wheeler you were following."

"Hope you didn't mind."

"Not at all. What kind of bike are you pulling?"

"A 1960 Harley flathead," Jeremiah said.

"A real classic," the man said.

"Yes, it is."

"Where you headed?"

"Brandon," Jeremiah said. "You?"

"Winnipeg. And it's not getting any closer with me standing here jawing. I'd better get to it. I'm going to try and drive out of it. Nice to meet you. You drive safe."

"You, too," Jeremiah said.

The man walked away, and Jeremiah pulled the book he was reading from his backpack and settled in to wait out the storm.

An hour later, he was back on the road. Visibility had improved, and the snow had slackened considerably. Traffic was light and the roads passable. Everything considered, Jeremiah was fortunate. He made good time while finishing his book on CDs. He checked in to a Best Western in Brandon, Manitoba, soon after dark. He ordered a small pizza and a large

Diet Coke from Pizza Express and was pleasantly surprised at how good his meal was. After eating, he texted Youngblood:

A snowstorm adventure. Safe in Brandon, Manitoba. Final destination tomorrow. Hello to Mary. Blessings.

Don texted back immediately:

Good to hear from you. T. Elbert has feeling in his left foot. Stay safe.

Jeremiah smiled and thanked God. *What great news!* He never knew when someone might be healed or improved when he was around. He tried to read but couldn't.

During his nighttime prayers, he again gave thanks for the news about T. Elbert and prayed for his continued healing. Fifteen minutes later, Jeremiah was sound asleep.

That night, the angel came to Jeremiah in a dream so real that he might as well have been in the motel room. Or maybe he was. It so hard to tell. "Go with God's blessing," the angel said, "and claim what you seek. You have earned your reward, and you deserve a rest. It may be a long time before you hear from me again."

37

Five days after New Year's

Today was the big day. Jeremiah's emotions were running high. Excitement, fear, anxiety, and anticipation were all coursing through his body. As he prayed for a sense of peace and calm that morning, he began to settle down.

He skipped breakfast and was on the road early. He crossed into Saskatchewan. Midmorning, he picked up a breakfast sandwich and coffee in the small town of Indian Head. He ate while driving.

That afternoon, with the address from Don Youngblood programmed into his GPS, Jeremiah drove to Moose Jaw, a small town with a population of nearly thirty-five thousand. He came in from the south on Highway 2, which became Main Street when he crossed into the city limits. The town looked alive, and he could imagine he might like to stay awhile. Just north of Route 1, the Trans-Canada Highway, Jeremiah drove out of Moose Jaw into the northern countryside. Not long afterward, he turned off Highway 2 onto a side road that led him to the address he sought.

At the bottom of the driveway, he looked up the gentle slope to a beautiful, large A-frame home. The house looked well cared for. Snow was on the ground, but the driveway was clear. Jeremiah saw a large parking area and a three-car garage. The main entrance was to the left of the garage. He pulled to the top and maneuvered the van so it was pointing out toward the road. He got out and stood still for a moment, then climbed the few stairs to the front door.

He was about to press the doorbell when it opened. He couldn't believe his eyes. Jeremiah knew she had to be almost eighty years old, but she didn't look a day over forty. *She's still gorgeous*, he thought.

When she realized who he was, her hand went to her mouth in sheer amazement. "Oh, my God," Linda Street said. "Jerry, it's you!"

"It's Jeremiah now," he said. In school, he had never told anyone his given name. He was named after his grandfather but was always called Jerry. As far as he knew, only his birth certificate and driver's license bore the name Jeremiah. Now, he embraced it.

Linda paused and studied him. "Jeremiah," she said. "It's perfect. I never knew. I love it."

He's more handsome than ever, Linda thought. She came out on the stoop and embraced him. He held her a long time. Tears streamed down Jeremiah's face, and Linda began to sob. When she settled down and raised her face to his, he stroked her hair and kissed her gently. She kissed him back. Then they kissed again, a longer kiss.

"I always knew you would come someday," she said. "And now that you're here, I can't believe it. Come in, come in."

✦ ✦ ✦

They sat side by side on barstools in the beautifully appointed kitchen.

"May I open a bottle of wine?" Linda said.

"That would be nice," Jeremiah said.

Linda uncorked a bottle of her favorite red blend and poured two goblets half full. She handed one to Jeremiah. "Welcome home," she said, hardly able to contain herself.

They touched goblets and drank.

"It's good to be here," he said.

"I have a thousand questions."

"I only have one," Jeremiah said.

"You first," Linda said.

"Will you marry me?"

"Absolutely," Linda said without hesitation. "The sooner, the better."

"Praise God," Jeremiah said. "I've waited years to ask that question."

"Speaking of years," Linda said, "what took you so long? Tell me your story, and then I'll tell you mine."

He drank some wine and took a moment to settle his thoughts. He had so much to tell. "Well, it all started when I died in a rock-climbing accident," Jeremiah began. Even limiting himself to the highlights, he talked almost nonstop for an hour. Linda hung on every word. He finished by saying, "So, Donald Youngblood somehow tracked you down, and here I am."

Linda slid off her barstool, came to Jeremiah, and kissed him passionately. The phrase "Kisses sweeter than wine" ran across his mind.

"You better get used to that," Linda said. "I've been waiting a long time."

"So have I," he said as she kissed him again.

They took the bottle of wine and some snacks and moved to the sun porch, which was winterized. The night was coming fast, and the snow outside had a luminous effect in the twilight. Jeremiah thought the view was spectacular, looking out across a wide valley with a snow-capped mountain range as a backdrop. He felt like he could stay in this place with Linda for a long time. He hoped that was possible.

"You look fabulous," he said. "You don't look a day over forty."

"A gift from you, I suspect," she said. "The night we made love for the one and only time, the night I seduced you, something happened. Something wonderful passed between us. I could feel it. It was glorious, but it frightened me. Whatever it was, I suspect it's the reason I'm aging so slowly. Are you sure you're not from another planet?"

"As far as I know, I'm an earthling."

They laughed.

"You haven't aged much either," Linda said. "You're more handsome than ever."

"Thank you," Jeremiah said. "So, fill me in on the last fifty-some years."

"I'll give you the short version and fill in the gaps later. I went off to college, as you know, and ended up with a master's degree in education."

"Harvard, right?"

"Yes."

"You never came home during the summer," Jeremiah said. "That always disappointed me."

"I had a job as a teaching assistant on campus with free room and board. I wasn't much interested in coming home. I was a bit of a snob in those days, but I never forgot about you. You haunted me. At that time, I didn't think we'd ever be together."

"I never forgot about you either. I always hoped I'd find you. Go on."

"I got a teaching job in Boston and stayed for twenty years," she said. "During that time, I got my doctorate. I dated, but nothing serious. When I started getting Fountain of Youth jokes on a regular basis, I decided it was time to move on. I didn't want to become a lab rat. I went to California and got a professorship at the University of San Francisco. Everybody looks young in California, so I didn't draw too much attention. I did things to make myself look older—dressed old, didn't wear makeup, like that. After twenty years at USF, I retired. I decided I wanted to move to Canada. I did a lot of research online, then one day I found this house. I came up to have a look and fell in love with it. Money wasn't an issue. My parents both passed within a year of each other and left me well off. I made a cash offer on the house, and they accepted. I never thought I'd stay this long, but I love it here. I have no plans to leave, especially now."

"Never got married?"

"No," she said.

"Why?"

"I knew you'd come back to me someday."

"How did you know?"

"You told me," Linda said, smiling.

"I did?"

"In a dream. More than once. Always the exact same dream. You're walking away from me, and you turn and look back over your shoulder, and you say, 'I'll be back. It may be awhile, but I'll be back.' And you walk away and disappear into thin air. It's so real." She was crying again. "I knew you'd come someday. I just cannot believe you're actually here. It's a miracle."

EPILOGUE

I often refer to that January after Jeremiah left as the month of the three miracles.

The week after T. Elbert felt me poking his left foot with a fork, I took him to see Evan Smith. A CAT scan confirmed the beginning of healing in T. Elbert's spine. Evan had no explanation, other than it was another miracle. He had seen and heard so much recently, he just accepted it. Two weeks later, T. Elbert moved his left foot. He was convinced he would walk again, especially after I played the tape of my conversation with Jeremiah. I played the tape because I wanted him motivated.

Miracle number two was a phone call from Roy. Joseph Fleet had called from Florida. A recent visit to his doctor revealed his brain tumor had disappeared. They gave credit to the treatment. I knew better.

The final January miracle was in my own personal world. I took Jake to the vet for his annual checkup. He was already one of the oldest standard poodles on record, and I was concerned he wouldn't be around much longer. After I waited for an hour, the vet called me into his office.

"What have you done to this dog?" he said.

"What do you mean?"

"I mean, whatever you're doing, keep doing it. If I didn't know Jake personally, I'd think he was seven or eight years old. He looks much younger than the last time I saw him. At this rate, he might make the *Guinness Book of World Records* for oldest standard poodle ever."

God bless you, Jeremiah, I thought.

✦ ✦ ✦

On the first day of February, I sat at my usual table in the Mountain Center Diner and played the tape of my conversation with Jeremiah James for Billy. Billy had come to town to do a photo shoot. He ate slowly while listening to the tape.

"And the bullet that was stopped by the Yeti," Jeremiah said as the tape neared its end, "that wasn't blind luck. You were, and are, being protected. You have much work left to do. The battle between good and evil will not stop until the end of the age. You and Mary will live long and happy lives together and keep many people from harm."

I pressed the stop button. "That's it," I said.

"Interesting," Billy said. "Who else has heard this?"

"Mary and T. Elbert," I said. "What do you think?"

"No reason not to believe it," Billy said, "especially given what you've told me about T. Elbert and Joseph Fleet. And, of course, Jake."

"Did Jeremiah do the window paintings I saw on Main Street?"

"Yes, he did," I said.

"He's very creative. And talented. How long did it take him to do the diner's window?"

"Don't know," I said.

"He did each store in one night," Doris said as she arrived and set down our food. "Sorry, couldn't help overhearing the question. The diner was first. He did twelve storefronts in all."

"Like the twelve days of Christmas," I said.

"Or the twelve tribes of Israel," Billy said.

"I wouldn't know about that," Doris said. "But all the owners have agreed to leave them on their windows for the month of January. You-all enjoy your breakfast." Doris hurried away.

"It's been a long time since I heard anyone mention the twelve tribes of Israel," I said. "If you can name them all, I'll be really impressed."

Billy looked at me and smiled. "Asher, Benjamin, Dan, Gad, Issachar, Judah, Joseph, Levi, Naphtali, Reuben, Simeon, and Zebulun."

"You went to Sunday school as a child," I said. "You memorized them in alphabetical order."

"I did," Billy said. "My adoptive parents were very spiritual. We went to a Methodist church every week. I memorized a number of scriptures, the books of the Bible, and the twelve tribes of Israel. I also memorized

"I believe it one hundred percent," I said. "There are too many coincidences for it not to be true."

"The truth has a way of revealing itself no matter what," Billy said. "Our knowledge of the universe is like a drop of water in the ocean, the drop being our knowledge and the ocean being what we don't know."

"I get it, Chief," I said. "We have to accept some things on faith."

"We do," Billy said. "When's the last time you heard from him?"

"He texted me the Saturday morning after New Year's. The text read; *the eagle has landed. Results spectacular.*"

"A man of few words," Billy said. "Did you get the meaning?"

"I did," I said. "A few days later, I had another text. One word; *Married.*"

Billy smiled widely. "Good for him. He went looking for his dream girl and found her. You and I can relate."

"Yes, we can relate," I said. "And yes, good for him."

✦ ✦ ✦

Jeremiah's artwork on the storefront windows was washed away in the early days of February, but not before Billy Two-Feathers took photos of all the windows from different angles for a local writer.

The writer had decided to do a book about this past Christmas in Mountain Center. The book was titled *That Special Christmas*. It featured the best of the storefront window photos, one from each store. It also included pictures of the live Nativity, pictures of the carved Nativity, and stories about why it was such a special Christmas. The stories were submitted by Mountain Center residents. Most prominent were stories by Dr. Evan Smith and Pastor Adam Church. Many of the stories included the stranger in town and all the good things he did: Jeremiah James, the Christmas Stranger.

Merry Christmas!

AUTHOR'S NOTE

I went straight from finishing *Three Doorways Dark* to writing *The Christmas Stranger*. My wife, Tessa, had hounded me for years to write a Youngblood Christmas story. I wasn't interested. Then, for some reason, there it was, begging to be told.

I finished this book in a month, give or take a few days. Unprecedented. I couldn't stay away from my computer. I started with the bar scene at the Bloody Duck and just rolled with it. The story took over. I had no control over it.

As I write this author's note we are weeks away from seeing *Three Doorways Dark* as a finished book. A month later we will see *The Christmas Stranger*.

Note to self: Never again try to publish two books at once. I had a hard time keeping up with who said what in which book.

✦ ✦ ✦

As this Christmas book heads for the finish line, Covid -19 has reared its ugly head in the form of the Delta variant, fueled by those who refuse, for whatever reason, to be vaccinated. The press is full of stories of the unvaccinated who are now dead. I pray you are not one of those people.

Do not make going unvaccinated a political statement. It's not worth it. Do not be influenced by the media and social networks. Please, talk to a qualified doctor or nurse and make the right decision for yourself.

Be careful out there and stay safe.

✦ ✦ ✦

May this Christmas season be a special one for you and yours.

ACKNOWLEDGMENTS

My thanks to:

My wife, Tessa who fussed over the proofing of this book with the love and care of a mother hen sitting on her nest.

Steve Kirk whose eye for detail and unabashed honesty, always make my books better than they would have been. I take it as a good sign that you did not leave much of this one in your recycle bin. Eight books and counting, Steve!

Todd Lape, Lape Designs in Madison, MS for another great looking jacket and text design. Ten books and counting, Todd. Always a pleasure.

Meri Saffelder, our web master. Thank you for caring for the Donald Youngblood Mysteries website with skill and professionalism.

Mary Sanchez, publicist and friend. Youngblood Nation salutes you for all your hard work.

Buie Hancock at *Buie Pottery* who has supported Youngblood Nation from the beginning and given

Donald Youngblood a presence in Gatlinburg, TN. Drop in or visit www.buiepottery.com.

Dr. Glen Moody at *I Love Books* Bookstore, Kingsport, TN who has given Donald Youngblood a home in the Fort Henry Mall. Stop by and say Youngblood sent you.

Book lovers everywhere, especially Youngblood fans; buy books!